The Sanguinaires

Or What I Hate Most About Everything

The Sanguinaires
Or What I Hate Most About Everything

Gabriel Verveniotis

QUATTRO BOOKS

The publication of THE SANGUINAIRES has been generously supported by the Canada Council for the Arts and the Ontario Arts Council.

Canada Council for the Arts Conseil des arts du Canada

ONTARIO ARTS COUNCIL
CONSEIL DES ARTS DE L'ONTARIO
an Ontario government agency
un organisme du gouvernement de l'Ontario

Cover painting: Caitlin Walton
Cover design and typography: Jared Shapiro
Editor: Rob Shoub

Library and Archives Canada Cataloguing in Publication

Verveniotis, Gabriel, author
The sanguinaires : or, What I hate most about everything / Gabriel Verveniotis.

ISBN 978-1-988254-46-3 (softcover)

I. Title. II. Title: What I hate most about everything.

PS8643.E7795S26 2017 C813'.6 C2017-905907-6

Published by Quattro Books Inc.
Toronto, Canada
www.quattrobooks.ca

Printed in Canada

One

The Meeting

Forced religious conversions
Irregularly inspected Ferris wheels
Realizing you don't like any of your friends

HERE I am again on a Monday night... a dismal shanty of a church wallowing in the murky underbelly of Toronto's Annex. I'm condemned to a hollowed-out basement that once hosted a suggestion of hope. Now it's littered with leaflets for salsa night every other Tuesday and the up-and-coming "excitement" of Thursday's kid's choir practice.

IT'S funny how the entire extent of the West's ambition to Christianize the world can be reduced to this rubble of architectural excrement, the interior of which is blessed with photocopied promotional pamphlets of Spaniards doing the tango – or salsa, whatever the fuck the difference is...

IN more recent times, this aborted refuge of a church exclusively facilitated AA meetings and food services to the squalid miasmal creatures of the street – a more noble vocation than Christendom now that I think about it. It seems today to be catering more towards our growing collection of ragtag "Sanguinaires," whose only consolation is in discussing the one thing we're not supposed to mention.

"HELLO there and welcome, how are we all doing tonight? As most of you already know, my name is Ronald and I am a

Rectified Sanguinaire." A choir of cultish fervor erupted with the churned-out repetition of the announcer's name, "Hi, Ronald!" The speaker nodded to the group.

HE continued, "I hope you've all taken the week to practice the thought exercises we talked about at our last meeting so that we're on the same page for this evening's plan. Before we get to the main topic, though, I'd like to make some announcements.

AS you may have heard, this room will be occupied next Thursday by the 'Life for Life' children's choir practice, so we're going to have to make use of the boiler room that day."

THE room forfeited any medieval charm that might have redeemed its sterile ambience. The Department had ransacked what was left of religion's skid mark and confiscated its remains. All things considered, what went on within the walls of the church varied very little despite the Department's takeover – it wasn't like any prayer was going on before the collapse of Christendom, and the rest of those other religions...

THE speaker began again after a short pause with a contrived glint in his eye, "I do have some good news, though. I'm happy to announce that we are now allowed to share the coffee machine with upstairs, and I'm going to have a word with the Department and try to convince them that despite the renovations to the boiler room, it still may not be safe. Then again, we can't really expect more than one blessing in a week," he said, smiling like a moron.

COME to think of it now, the boiler room wasn't much worse than the room we were in, with its snot-cream-coloured walls and checkered floors which featured a puke-like green as an accent on every other tile. But the boiler room did have one thing we were missing... one of the construction workers must have had a flair for aesthetics, because he'd put up this picture of a little boat scuttling through the high seas. I wouldn't be surprised if that's what had made the room habitable enough for the Department to sanctify it for its new usage.

BACK to the jabbering idiot... Ronald was the kind of guy whose character, countenance and impression on others was less colourful than a wood-washed spare bedroom from the early 1990s. Even now I find it stagnating to describe a personality that defies any hint of particularity or distinctiveness.

I guess you could say he was most akin to the space beneath someone's table: a sort of overlooked middle ground that lurks in the beneath of life's abundant and active grandiosity. But who am I to denigrate a Rectified group leader? He seemed to know enough not to be sitting where I was, which often led me to question how he ever became a Sanguinaire...

HE kept blathering on, "Now back to tonight's lesson... Hmmm... ah yes, I was like all of you once, troubled by the same affliction... if you could call it that. When I was an active Sanguinaire like yourselves, I refused to confront the challenges of my life without seeing the Event behind everything. It was like a perpetual gloom that permeated every thought, idea and feeling I had about anything. This destroyed my ambitions, my ability to love or be loved, and my drive to participate in society. I was obsessive and couldn't for the life of me feel or think about anything else."

I'D heard this diatribe of his before, and every time I listened to it I played a little game with myself to try and catch where he'd repeat the same intonations at the most effective points in his soliloquy. That night I noticed a few new faces in the group. I hated any time there were new skids because it meant this idiot would have to inspire us more forcefully with his lacklustre tale of overcoming adversity and finding himself.

WHY is it that these "profound" moments of wisdom and "true" revelations are also the most forced and formulaic? If there was just one iota of reality to these fucking stories we wouldn't feel so cheated and cheap after listening to these hucksters. Instead it always comes off as a kitschy sound bite with undertones of persecutory pomp, the kind you'd hear from a once-overweight coach who now takes pride in parading his average new figure and daring accomplishments to a bunch of students that just want to get high behind the janitor's shed.

I noticed Ronald posing in this awkwardly limp fashion, trying to appear lax and casual; oh, it was measured and repulsive... Ronald continued: "I clung to the Event as you all do, thinking that if I let it go I'd be deceiving myself, or abandoning my one and only hope of making sense out of it. Most Sanguinaires believe that their obsession with the Event is natural and necessary. I know you all feel unique for being able to read into this phenomenon the way you have so far, but it's just not healthy.

I also know how tempting it is to believe that there is something we can do to change it. I too felt and believed this, for real, guys – we're all here for the same reason. I found ways to tolerate the affliction because I thought it was my only chance to take charge of my own destiny. The reality, however, was that I was suffocating myself in a swamp of my own creation. Remember, guys, there is never a good reason to make yourself feel depressed. Coming around to this fact is what allowed me to understand what Rectification is all about, and now look at me – I'm an instructor, as you can see!"

HE carried on, "At first I relied on medication but, like many of you, I soon realized that I was resistant in almost every way. With the medical route exhausted, I gradually began to accept the importance of groups like this one, and that's when I started to find something meaningful in Rectification therapy. Thankfully I never became radicalized, or I'm sure it would have been a lot harder... Do any of you have any questions?" the speaker asked rhetorically, just so you couldn't say he hadn't tried to create a 'dialogue'.

ONE of the members must have been gullible enough to partially swallow this vomit, and he asked, "I don't know, Ronald… how can we just come to terms with… how do we find a way to adjust to something like this?"

"THAT'S a good question," answered the group leader. "I saw the light after attending these very meetings, but that's only one way. I learned just by listening, and over time these classes allowed me to see that the Event was not anything transcendent or inexplicable. I slowly started to see that it was nothing more than a treatable cognitive dysfunction. I learned to simply accept that the Event had happened. Easy as that. Any further examination is unproductive at best, and at worst it's very harmful. And this, my brave tadpoles, is why Rectification therapy is so important. This is why you all need to be pragmatic, to strive to get where I am. In this way we can overcome your delusions together."

ANOTHER member of our forlorn group felt annoyed enough to blurt something out, "That's easy for you to say! You're on the Department payroll. Besides, what if we don't wanna get doped up and prostitute ourselves out for the D.P.W.? Is that all we get to look forward to? Prescriptions and your sad version of recovery?!"

RONALD rebuked the fellow sharply: "Medication is only one part of being Rectified, and obviously we can see that this form of treatment is not always a viable one. Darius," he said to the anemic boy/man who had interrupted, "I'm just like you. I wouldn't be hosting these sessions if it didn't affect me as much as it does you. So don't think we're not on the same page, okay, son? No one is trying to force medication on you, we just want you to know that it's an option and, between us, it's being worked on and improved as we speak.

THE Department's task is to find out why and how Sanguinaires and dogmatized religious groups are resistant to the medication. That's what I and the rest of the team leaders are here to observe and resolve, so be patient and cooperate."

RONALD forced his eyebrows down in a pathetic attempt to look concerned and disheartened. This was followed by a spewing of some sentimental sonnet about the perilous life he'd led before the light of treatment had dawned upon him. "It was hard for me… hard, I swear. I went in circles looking for answers and got nowhere.

BUT we need to just accept the Event, to understand that it just is. It's unapproachable, so there's no need to feud with ourselves. It just happened, and it's okay to admit that and to let go..."

"GO fuck yourself! Really, it just happened?! That's all, bit of therapy and be patient?" sputtered a ruddy member of the congregation.

RONALD responded to him with insipid patience: "Do I need to remind you again that your attempts to trigger our safe space are not welcome? We've spoken about this before. You need to refrain from aggravating the group and using unsafe language that may offend some of us. I see that someone didn't go over their mental exercises this week."

HE dished out the last little reprimand with the aegis of an elementary school teacher. The group leader then began the Sanguinaire slogan for us to all repeat:

"WHAT cannot be changed will not be changed. Things will be as they will be. I am powerless to control this, but I am on the path to empowered understanding."

THE aforementioned instigator of our classroom revolution responded after we were done our little chant, "Go fuck yourself, Ronald!"

RONALD took a deep, forced breath, more of an exaggerated gesture than a need to actually gain air and composure. The loud wisecracker took the opportunity to continue, "I don't see how you can sit there peddling this smarmy little plot of yours, trying to make us forget what happened, I can't and won't forget, fuck you!"

OUR Rectification leader tried to interrupt but couldn't get a word in – the rabble-rouser just carried on, "I'll tell ya what's what, bucko! There's a reason, a plot, goddammit! That's why we're resistant to those fucking little poppers the Department and its pharmaceutical lackeys keep dishing out!"

RONALD made a lame effort to stop him but it was no use.

"THE Event didn't just happen, and it for sure didn't come outta nothing! You understand, ya goof? I'll tell it to ya straight, nothing doesn't just come from nothing, there's always a rhyme or reason for everything that's ever been, there's a beat to it all, and we gotta start figurin' it all out, not forgetting! It all came from somewhere... something higher, can't you see that? Am I the only one who's got the balls to say what we all went through? We all know it's true, for fak's sake – what's it gonna take for you to admit to your own bullshit?!"

THE interrupting agitator was in his late forties. I'd seen him at meetings before and knew he went by the classy name of 'Cooter'. Cooter was the boisterous type, and if ever the expression "shoot first and ask questions later" were to apply, surely it would find a home as his epithet. His face was checkered by former acne scars, as well as a host of other battle wounds that seemed only to enhance his countenance. He was a rugged nobody. He had a swagger to him that was uncouth but still agreeable somehow. Despite his unruly temperament, he appeared to possess an aptitude for the questioning of higher things, which is more than I can say for ninety percent of the rubes I'm forced to cower from on a daily basis.

"YEAH, that's right!" exclaimed Darius, the first member of the group who'd spoken up that day.

COOTER was encouraged. "Thank you! Someone here still gives a shit. Which is more than I can say for you, Ronald, and probably for the rest of ya," he finished, snarling at the crowd like a scrappy mutt with the scent of blood at its nose.

RONALD was upset by this point and found solace in his reliable set of stock phrases: "You need to relax. Do not get so carried away. You're giving in to the mania of your disorder. This is exactly what I am trying to help you with. Why won't you let me help you?"

RONALD looked open-eyed toward the group. "You see, guys, what we have here is a clear example of the dangers of this mental impairment. It's a cancer that cripples sensible discourse and upsets balanced temperaments."

HE went on, "I know it's upsetting, and it's a big part of what we need to work on overcoming. That's why I'm not mad at you, Cooter; I understand. But your inability to move past the Event is unhealthy, and if you don't make a real effort towards Rectification soon, you may never be able to lead a regular, healthy life."

I could tell Ronald was peeved despite his charade of calmness, but he managed to adopt a parental hubris as he delivered his patronizing blow: "I hope that we can find a way to help you, Cooter, but considering how disruptive you've been today, I'm going to have to ask you to leave and resume your sessions next week."

"WHY?" the agitator asked.

"BECAUSE you have violated our safe-space policy."

COOTER responded with genuine curiosity, "What are you talking about? This whole situation is unsafe."

IN reply, Ronald began to roll out all his little rules: "Ahem, the Department and its enumerated policies stipulate that we can't have this kind of riotous and provocative behaviour. While you are free to think as you wish, we ask that you refrain from using incendiary language that may upset others in therapy.

I'M sorry, Cooter, but we can't make exceptions for this kind of conduct. You can return next week, though, and I won't tell your employer or your home supervisor about this little incident, nor will I make a formal charge pertaining to your violation of the radicalization policy." The group leader was finished. He sneered down at his embarrassed foe, basking in the perfume of victory.

COOTER shimmied himself maliciously off his seat, and before charging through the door, he looked at Ronald and gave him a final scolding. "You fucking-little-mole rat, all you can do is cower into a safe hole of 'policies' – will they block out the vision…? Will they change or make any sense outta the Event?!" The room reverberated with a myriad of mixed responses. "You stand there, hiding behind your tablet, dishing out sermons 'bout what's real and what isn't. You bog down on guys like me for having the balls to stare it right in the face and follow through where you failed!"

WITH this outburst, Cooter strode heroically out of the church basement, leaving most of the group in an uproar of resurfaced enthusiasm to talk about the Event.

Two

After the meeting

Free giveaways that you don't actually want
Baseballs thrown through windows
Beached whales

THE meeting eventually settled down and then concluded, as usual, with a drab and drudging exodus to our respective hollow elsewheres. I went outside and noticed Cooter leaning on a corner of the church, smoking a cigarette in this James Dean-like pose. I suspect he fancied himself a little like Dean because he wore this tight, off-red jacket, but in reality he was more like an aged, gin-soaked Bogart, straight from the ruins of *The African Queen*.

I gathered that he was still swilling the aftertaste of undigested contempt in his mouth. The only thing I could say for this guy was that he still cared...

"HIYA!" I heard him but didn't make eye contact. "You over there, sailor in the grey coat, you look familiar. I know I've seen you shuffling around this shithole lately. Come have a smoke," the faux revolutionary pressed.

I figured he'd noticed me noticing him. There's nothing worse than knowing someone in some slight capacity and then being forced to associate with them beyond the comfortable context of that initial collision of selves... Ah well... "Hey, um... Cooter, right?"

OF course I knew his fucking name! That's another thing I hate, when two people perform this gaudy tap dance of tailored aloofness, both feigning ignorance and uncertainty, and all the while each is painfully aware of the other's name, friends, exes, bad habits...

"YEAH, it's Sir Cooter Squith to you, pal! You gonna have a smoke or what?"

I looked at him hesitantly and replied, "I'll come for a stand."

MR. Squith asked, befuddled, "What's a stand?"

FOR some reason I felt like answering him truthfully, which is a rare thing for me, "Well, I don't smoke, but I'm pro-smoker. Given the nature of our situation, how could anyone even pretend to care about secondhand smoke? Besides, the way I see it is people tend to bond over smoking. It creates a group and a reason for strangers to stand and inhale poisonous fumes off each other. I've noticed that people hate having to communicate without an excuse of this kind. So I think it's nice."

COOTER joined in, "It's funny how even after the cards have been laid out, people still make a fuss about that kinda shit."

I nodded in agreement then paused... something strange was happening... I felt like getting into my theories on everything with this bum. Understand, I despise good form and resist executing compulsory courtesies with all my might. But there was something about this guy that seemed rotten and raw... I guess his temper made me remember a time when I cared too, so I went with it.

"IT makes this kinda ingroup and outgroup experience, and leaves the outgroup in the smoke-free dust of the ingroup's comradeship."

"GOOD point, but it'll kill ya'," grumbled the unkempt ruffian after huffing another toxic cloud of translucent fumes.

A ridiculous thing for him to say post-Event, but I carried on the dialogue: "Well sure, it's both corrosive and poisonous, but I couldn't care less for my health."

I continued, "You want to know what bothers me about those pro-health lobbyists? It's the public lynching they threaten you with for not signing up to their cause. I don't piss on them for wasting all that time and energy on the groundskeeping of those cadaverous tombs they call bodies. Why, then, must they spew such venom on anyone outside of their designated healthy-living camp? And Christ, do they love to scold the smokers. You guys are seen as these leprous creatures, out to contaminate every child's nursery, school or playground that lies in your wake. I swear to God, even a diddler's perversions get chalked up to an uncontrollable mental condition, but smokers, you poor devils are forever cast from the sympathetic realm of public understanding by the volition of your sins."

COOTER gave out another exhalation of smoke accompanied by a big laugh. "Well, that's a funny way to look at it. I just always figured they were right."

"THEY are right," I replied. "They just don't need to be so smug about it..."

HE laughed again, harder this time, and then I couldn't help but ask: "So what was going on back there at the meeting?"

COOTER popped his jacket collar up and started cleaning his teeth with a chipped nail he'd ripped off his finger; after a brief pause, he responded, "I'll tell you the whole tale over a beer. What say you, sailor, care for some grog?"

"ABSOLUTELY!" I didn't need any persuasion to accept the invitation... in that I was a semi-professional alcoholic and took the discipline quite seriously.

AND so we departed on a nautically inspired enterprise, searching out the welcoming embrace of a downtown Toronto bar. I've always seen bars as a sort of seaport in which stumbling patrons can gather from across the vast oceans of our cityscape. They are the stomping grounds of travelers from every specialty, vocation and walk of life. There, in the bar, one can find everyone and everything. It is a hub of sin, be it a dank and sordid cesspool, or a posh parlor with pompous would-be marquis fluttering about with their dapper gentlemen's garb and refined styles of elocution. Scurvy-tainted hoodlums can be spotted in hidden corners, while flush businessmen stand brashly at the helm. A bar's very interior gives one the impression of some darkened sea-hull and brings one into the mindset of a filthy but elated seaman…

FORGIVE me this romanticization. When the world you see is one of unrelenting ugliness and discord, it becomes mandatory to scribble over it with the small and weakened wonders of a tired imagination…

WE walked along College Street until we stumbled upon a whole slew of unsavory opportunities. Our arrival was awaited by the outstretched arms of the patios littering Augusta Avenue. There were siren-like maidens at one bar, harpie-type spitfires at another, and they all meshed together in one besotted stream of delirium, despair… and a promise of momentary ecstasy.

THE destination we approached was one of the harpy taverns. This ragged fortress of soullessness had a sort of used-condom charm about it, something that said 'needles are welcome here', and it demanded an audience from these two shipwrecked alcoholics.

COOTER nodded curtly in the dump's direction. "Let's head into that flophouse, looks like a worthy saloon."

WE sat down in the lugubrious hut of putrefying squalor. This was where dreams went to die. The waitress noticed us as we came in and meandered in our direction with a hostile temperament. I suppose we were pandering too much cheer and gentrifying the foul ambience of the venue. I couldn't complain, though; the beer was cheap and the characters were well worth the experience, especially our server who strongly resembled Rhea Pearlman.

SHE looked like a Scarlet, or maybe a Charlene. She staggered over to us with her upward-curled, acid-washed hair, resembling something from Mötley Crüe. She had lathered on red lipstick in a clown-like fashion and accompanied it with oh-so-complimentary pink and purple eye makeup, the absence of which would have thrown off much of her delicately crafted appeal.

"WHATCHA having, sweethearts?" I had been banking on her calling us darlin's, but sweethearts was close enough.

AMUSED, Cooter replied with an impish grin, "We'll have two of your finest lagers, and by finest I mean cheapest." She responded with a smoke-choked, "Cheers, guys," and sauntered on back from whence she came.

COOTER and I then exchanged a quick glance and fell into a fit of laughter, which might have set a nice tone for the evening had we not been so miserably afflicted by our 'Sanguinaire condition'.

THEN again, if it wasn't for this disorder of ours, we might not have felt compelled to spend time in this darling tavern in the first place. I suppose every mound of shit is worth digging through to find even the smallest nugget of gold, and who better to prospect with than a hopeless whelp even more fucked than I? As Schopenhauer once said, the only universal satisfaction in life is in knowing that someone else is either lower or worse off than you are.

AND so we entered into the evening; we were as two voyagers drifting down the Congo River, passing by a vantage point from which to view the dark and strange places that the heart of this city had to offer. Respite tastes like a flat beer poured from rusted taps...

Three

The *Event*, or How We Became Sanguinaires

School janitors with pedophiliac tendencies
Having to praise bad cooking
Lectures from strangers

HAVING looked around and taken in the specimens lurking in the huddled gloom, I took a swig and asked my new companion, "So, what happened in there today? You got awfully disgruntled at the meeting."

SMASHING his glass down, Cooter launched into an outburst of profanity-laden philosophy: "I'm just so fucking sick of spending week after week with these 'Rectified' varmints gettin' all doped on the Department's predilections! They feel like they got the right to preach their little sermons 'bout self-denial and forgetting how to feel.

ALL their sideways roundabouts and quick-talk about the same bullshit… there's no meaning to any of it! I mean, think about it, people have been waiting for a sign like this since the dawn of civilization, and when it finally bonks them on the head, they all go silent as if nothing's happened, and now the whole thing's too offensive to even mention!"

I had to ask, "So what? You think it was God that caused the Event?"

HE replied, "Shucks, I don't know… all I'm saying is that what or whoever caused it did so for a reason, and don't you think it's our job to figure out what it is? Let's be straight here, there's gotta be something about us that keeps us unaffected by the meds, something that lines up with our instinct to figure this shit out."

TALKING about the Event was an awkward taboo, akin to the subject of a dead relative. It was something no one cared to discuss. It had already happened, the result was the result, and there was no point pursuing the thing any further. People just got hurt or became closed off... but most of all they just got offended.

THE Event, like every other disconcerting aspect of life, was relegated to the realm of the unspoken. It existed as a bad smell that every once in a while seeped out from under a closed bathroom door, as if to say, "I can't be flushed! Get used to me." Known by all but never brought up, because no one wanted to offend the host who hadn't gotten around to repairing the latrine. I guess people felt that if it didn't help anyone or do any good to talk about it, why bother? No one would stop you if you did, but they likely wouldn't care much for your company afterwards…

I suppose it's high time we dabble for a moment in the grand maddening pool of mystery that is the Event. Well, it began with a cosmic epiphany, or maybe a kind of mental tumor of sorts. In a very real sense, the skies opened up and out poured this collective revelation, leaving momentary chaos in its wake. Ultimately, though, the whole ordeal only managed to inconvenience us as much as a delayed flight might, or the choppy lag of WiFi at a shitty café.

SOME years back, the entire world had an exact vision of how they were going to die.

ALL in synchronicity, all at the exact same moment… be it on the john or in the middle of a war zone, everyone knew when and how they had to go. They all caught the precognizant disease, as the Department likes to label it, and yet, if you looked around now, you'd never know it had even happened...

I guess it's the only time humans experienced a prophetic vision without the comfortable distance previously afforded by symbols and interpretation. There were no soaring doves carrying olive branches here. No flaming shrubs to subdue us gently into submission. No. This was an exact vision – clear and straight to the fucking point.

I'D have leapt at the chance to trade places with a lowly shepherd scooping the shit out of Abraham's flock, if it meant getting a vision of something as vague and peaceful as a land of milk and honey. Instead I got to see my cardiac arrest, and that couldn't be more annoying to know.

PRIOR to the Event, I could typically be found prancing around like a deranged baron, spouting highfalutin lessons on how best to live life. I was the dilettante of my time, campaigning against all of the world's oncoming traffic with the most belligerent assertions I could muster.

MY routine was really quite pleasant. I led an affable and incorrigible lifestyle with little to no reason for self-doubt or examination. I spent my free time socializing. I was a gregarious master on an island of self-imposed idleness, schmoozing my way in and out of conversations.

I had once held the honourable position of junior editor at a most respectable celebrity magazine, packing zingers galore into the highly reputable gossip column that occupied one of the corners of the internet. I was magnificent in this department. And it was here that I learnt the staunch objectivity that has stayed with me to this day. I devoted myself to the truth and resisted the temptation to sensationalize (a fault all too common in my trade). If his hair implants were obvious, they were described as such. But there was no cheap accompaniment of "What was he thinking???" If her husband was twenty years too young for her, then so it was written. But be assured I presented it as a fair and even twenty, and not the cruel twenty-five or thirty years you'd find in the columns of my misguided colleagues. I like to think I was respected for my honesty, but who knows?

REGARDLESS, I made more than decent money and I had a life… a base and deluded one perhaps, but a life that was my own. On the day of the Event, this all changed...

I was at a club when it happened. One of my coworkers had coerced me into going by dangling rumours of a pending promotion. I happily discovered that we were to be guests of honour that night, having a reservation in the VIP booths, and that bottle service was on the company's tab.

I soon found myself in a conversation with a club-conscripted floozy. Her name was Gloria. These types of ladies are usually hired to hover around desperate men and sometimes act as slutty consorts for their perverted and, more often than not, perpetually flaccid male employers. I knew Gloria could easily drink my wallet up without offering much in return. But what did I care? It wasn't my tab.

WE chitchatted a bit, first about music, I expressed my disdain for the musical epidemic that was today's rap scene, but to my surprise, my refined companion did not share my opinion. From there we somehow got on to the benefits of rhinoplasty. She told me she was thinking about getting some. I encouraged this.

"YOU know," I remarked, "it's actually considered a mark of distinction in certain Persian and Arabic countries, but only if the bandage is left on a little while after the surgery. That way everyone else knows you can afford it. Class is all in the nose, my dear."

WE went on like this for a bit until suddenly the music skipped and the DJ dropped to the floor, convulsing. At first I thought it was a seizure then realized it was much more likely an overdose. I chortled to myself and was just about to ask my companion if the prospect of drugs tickled her fancy, but she too dropped and began to twitch and writhe just as the DJ had.

IT wasn't long before I felt my own knees shake, and then I was hurled to the floor by an overwhelming impulse that seemed to override my motor functions. After that everything went black. Was I dead? Was this the void? Nothingness? I couldn't grasp what was going on or how long it went on for...

I felt like I was in a state of non-reality – just nothingness, and yet I was aware of my nothingness. After some indeterminate length of time, this phase stopped. I was myself. I took a gander around the club and noticed people shuffling absentmindedly; most of them had also stopped seizing.

THERE was a post-traumatic look to them all as they tried to get their bearings. As faces went from blank to bewildered, I began to experience a most lucid form of *déjà vu.* It crept in slowly and started to ferment in my consciousness. It was ethereal, fleeting, dreamlike and yet somehow cognizant. It felt like a memory on the cusp of being recalled, and yet it was fragmented. I guess it felt like the beginnings of a premonition, since that is what it was... I was in a stasis of panic; this thing was freezing me up, inhibiting all my thoughts and actions.

ALL at once, I had my vision. It was my death. It appeared to me as this poignant, vacuous image, half-clear yet encumbered by whatever mental and physical paralysis was affecting me. I felt this enormous pressure on my chest. It seemed malevolent in nature. It was like something was pressing down on my body, strangling me, suffocating me... I caught death's whiff and knew this was a terminal encounter.

I steadied myself repeatedly, trying to gain more control of the moment, of my experience. Little by little, my body became more relaxed, and the struggle to move around was dissipating. I was once again conscious of my surroundings. Everyone else in the club looked like they were still "in it," a bunch of heroin junkies nodding off, the needles still stuck in their arms. Vacant eyes enraptured by visions of death or something close to it. I felt terrified for them, hoping that they weren't still in whatever the fuck I had just got out of but knowing that they were. I turned to my companion and noticed her coming out of it.

I asked her what she thought had just happened; she responded by crying. I couldn't reach her, so I steadied myself a bit and decided to move around shaking people, trying to wake anyone I could, and gauge if we had all been on the same trip. The first guy I spoke to confirmed my worst fears… he didn't get into details, but it was enough for me to dispense with any further questioning of my own sanity.

EVERYONE started to stagger around the dance floor aimlessly. I was fortunate enough to retain the privileges afforded by my VIP seat; from there I could look over most of the plebeian wrestling pit of anxious faces.

GLORIA came to me and grabbed my hand, and for the first time in my juvenile life I held it with no desire to bend her over at some later point in the evening. I had no impulse to do or say anything that might pressure her into signing the contract of ardour, heretofore consummated by these very situations.

EVERYONE seemed to be hesitantly resuming whatever half-conscious outlook they may have previously held on the world, but I could see the signs of mortal affliction on them all. None of this was helped by the rancid smell that had accompanied the end of the seizures/visions: the reek of hardboiled eggs… eggs being repugnant enough in their snotty, bile-like sort of way, but hardboiled ones… disgusting, most disgusting!

THE DJ looked like a would-be shaman, with an actual pigeon feather fixed on his bonnet/bandana and an open chest decked out with turquoise painted hexagons surrounding an upside-down cross. He began to speak into the microphone, "Aiight gang, check it… I dunno wat jus' went down, but I'ma look ya'll in the face an' be say'n, honestly… honestly, WTF?"

HE enunciated each letter in the acronym with sincere befuddlement. If it weren't for everything about him, I would say I could empathize. Nevertheless, people for the first time had to confront the Event for what it was, myself included.

CONVERSATION by conversation, each of us confirmed that we all had something in common: a fear of confronting death. Bit by bit, the crowds began to question, muse and debate. No one could accept or believe that these episodes could be a vision of something as simple as the natural conclusion of all living things. Each person's dream was specific to their own end. It wasn't a shared vision of the same catastrophe but the realization of one's own personal meeting with the end. The apocalypse was within ourselves. Specific, individualized and unique, and yet experienced by us all, as a collective. It was something we now shamefully shared as a human race. I felt this and, for the first time, I was afraid.

DISCUSSION turned to argument, and arguments got rowdier as everyone, whether they liked it or not, had to get involved. Most avoided voicing their opinions right away. I, of course, couldn't help but delve head first into the controversy. However, I didn't possess the same verve as usual when it came to commenting on contentious subjects and experiences. The spark wasn't there, or maybe I wasn't there… all I could feel was the reality of the fact that I was going to die.

STILL, we slowly got into the meaty subjects, pondering the spiritual and metaphysical implications of our visions. At one point, an atheist in the group caught a whiff of the religious speculation going on. This made her mad and she took hold of the microphone, demanding that everyone return to the realm of reason: "Don't you guys get that whatever we experienced has a scientific explanation! Are you trying to tell me that some spaghetti monster gave you a peep into the other world?"

MOST people ignored her at first and she dropped the mic with an embarrassed shrug. There was a lot of suggestion going on that maybe this thing was inexplicable. An older, bald, mustached man did not want to take any opinion and was very opinionated about this. I believe he put it thusly: "Now, let's be straight here, I'm just as confused as everyone else. The difference is that I'm going to stay open to every possibility, we can't afford to be closed off."

THE microphone abandoner heard him and made another stand to pontificate her lack of a point: "Don't be afraid to think for yourselves, guys. There's an explanation, and it's always scientific for these kind of things, we just need to figure it out. I know some of you might still have some prehistoric views about the world but guess what, the spaghetti monster didn't create the world in six days and neither did she visit you today with a vision. Let's be sensible. Maybe our bodies are feeling the effects of all those pesticides we're constantly ingesting?!"

THE bald man just sighed. However, a lot of the club began to gravitate closer to this woman's tempting rhetoric; the lure of nonbelief has that kind of effect sometimes... The little imp managed to recruit a group of listeners that were now starting to surround her in a circle of fear, awe and a desire to be healed by sense and reason, both of which they believed were transmitting straight out of her yammering mouth.

THE fiend was delighted by all the attention and didn't miss the opportunity to take a selfie in front of the crowd and post it online. And within the hour, I was made aware that there was a fierce online war going on over what the Event was and how it affected us all.

IT was gross and I had no desire to participate in the zealous forum. I took my leave, bidding Gloria farewell and cementing the momentousness of this occasion by not even taking her phone number. I had to be alone with my thoughts and feelings about what I had just experienced.

I still remember my untimely demise like it was yesterday. There I was, just gasping for air, my heart collapsing into an abyss of panic, compounded by an even worse feeling of meta-remembrance and absolute forfeiture, knowing that I couldn't do a fucking thing to change any of it.

YOU'D think that having family around would make the end better, but now I know it's actually the complete opposite, because of how irreparably estranged you are from them. I know that they can't really hear, feel or fix you. They just stand there and stare back into your terrified eyes, reflecting a very different anguish from the one that you're experiencing – trust me, I remember… All the while you gaze back beseechingly…

painfully trying to determine what form of excruciation is more tolerable: the pain of watching others lose you or the feeling of being lost yourself.

THERE'S no such thing as a good death, death being the opposite of life – life being good because it's not death. It's fucking ugly, terrifying, simple as that. Enough of this, though; let's get back to Cooter…

"IN any case," I said to him, "what's there to accomplish by exasperating these Rectifiers? It's not like they're going to drop their stance on the whole issue and agree with us. And even if you were able to convince Ronald to confront whatever lame vision of death he had, what good would that do him? The guy found a way around our would-be affliction through therapy. Why does it matter that he cares? What does that say about the strength of your convictions if you don't feel certain unless everyone shares the same belief as you?

"DON'T get me wrong," I continued, "I'm still trying to make sense of this calamity just like you. I hate anyone who writes the Event off as a mental illness. I feel like a convicted felon forced to live in exile of truth, but I don't know if badgering these morons is going to bring about what we're looking for. The second you have to coerce someone into accepting your beliefs is the second those beliefs lose all credibility. The way I see it, you shouldn't need an audience to verify a truth…"

"NO!" Cooter interrupted, "I won't let this little Pontius Pilate swindle his way out of taking responsibility for what the Department's making us do! Registering us, institutionalizing us, fucking all of it. I can't even get a job anymore without clearing fucking psych inspections and monitoring my every word of speech, and it's all because of guys like Ronald. The middle man always thinks he's not at fault… I'll have him wash his hands in a sewer before he says they're clean." Cooter burped right after saying this, and in a funny way it helped his point.

“IT’S high time everyone begins to accept that they got a stake in this thing, no one’s exempt. I don’t believe there’s a single person who can say they weren’t affected by the Event, but no one even pretends to give a shit anymore… I know there’s still some of us out there! Everybody just walks around like it never happened, and it’s because we don’t speak up to guys like Ronald that this shit continues.”

FOR some reason, in that moment I began to suspect why Cooter might have taken such a shine to me. It struck me like a gentle, uninvited pat on the thigh from a stranger who, with his palm still pressed snug, raises one eyebrow and says, “Hey there, fella, how ’bout it?”

I replied violently, not to his words but to my realization, “I won’t be able to finish this beer if you think I’m a potential candidate for whatever backward religious mission you might be on. I can’t accept this experience as a part of some apocalyptic prophecy. Don’t cast the Event into a religious template. I don’t even want to start with why that’s problematic. I won’t ever accept it as a celestial message, so if that’s what you’re thinking, we’re through.”

THE silenced renegade took a swig and returned, “If you’re not looking at life through a religious lens, then what’s the point of even looking…? Listen, fella, the fact that we all had a vision – everyone, all at once – has to make you think that this thing is more than a maybe! You gotta ask yourself why it happened and for what reason. Fuck, man, if everyone would acknowledge once a month that it even happened, that would be a start!”

I tried to interrupt, “But…”

COOTER blitzkrieged my sentence before I could even begin, "Look here, pal, if God isn't a part of the question, then it isn't a question I wanna ask, because I have nothing to gain without his bargaining chip."

"IS that what God is to you, a good bet at Death's poker game?"

AND so I had discovered, after spending no more than a few hours with this character, that he knew how to stir up this inner anarchy in people... and it made me want to know more about him, despite his fanatically religious angle. Before I continue and get into our "fated" magnetism, however, I'd like to fill you in on why I took such an issue with the whole religion thing.

YOU see, after the Event, there was this kind of uproar of religious violence. It started soft and inquisitive, mostly through conversations like the one Cooter and I had just been having. But it grew. You can hardly blame them, though; overnight, almost every religious institution had experienced the satisfaction of receiving their long-awaited sign of the apocalypse... or salvation, whatever the fuck the difference is. It was too big a victory for them to handle gracefully. Religion was thrust into centre stage again – a place it hadn't occupied since the Dark Ages. For years it had been a dangling corpse: buried, dug up and held on display. Now believers felt powerful again. It went to their heads. And the world descended into riots. It was like an epilogue to an already forgotten piece of tragicomedy. Like watching your distant and forgotten relatives carnivorously skirmish through the putrefying leftovers of an inherited estate, all vying for the scraps of a once-prominent basis of dignity. Out came acts of terror and violence of almost every known variety.

DECAPITATIONS, bombings, mutilations. We witnessed it all. Nonetheless, the religious riots were short-lived uprisings, and in the end, the Event was responsible for religion's last big wail of relevance.

LOOKING back, I can almost understand why the Department is the way it is today. At the time, all their efforts were directed towards putting an end to this posthumous crusade of fanatical minds… In the end, it took the army to stop them.

EVENTUALLY, after we had all proven our collective hatred and propensity towards violence, some kind of agreement was reached that it couldn't go on like this, and steps were taken to establish the post-Event world of today. People felt that we had to accept the same set of principles that all nations could make an effort to enforce. We all recognized a mutual interest in obtaining the same societal results… and that is how the Department of Psychological Welfare (the D.P.W.) came to be.

THE government found a way to prevent future uprisings by investing more judicious power into the psychological branch of the public health department. This was the ploy they used to exercise their will… to override faith…

THE Department was able to circumvent laws and constitutions, and to impose ideological restrictions on those who favoured any values and beliefs that could be construed as obsessive, fanatical or radical. They managed to muscle themselves into a position of control by maintaining that the Event had been a part of some collective mental illness, an infection of the psyche.

THE Department wasn't necessarily tyrannical, but it did preside over the health and safety of its constituents, and in this capacity it was capable of overturning basic human rights.

THE D.P.W. shut down most major religious centres, starting with the Vatican and finishing up in Mecca. Governments granted them the authority to declare public religion a breeding ground for fanaticism and radicalism. But the Department took it one step further and began to target any philosophy that promoted a strict point of view on what the Event meant, or how we should live our lives after having experienced it. Last but not least, they refitted our local churches and other religious centres to facilitate the introduction of a new kind of therapy: Rectification Therapy.

FROM that day to this, global Rectification centres administered group sessions, geared to quell every thought, feeling and anxiety society had toward their experience of the Event. Most depressing of all, the Department found a way to semi-legalize the mandatory ingestion of a medication called Nepenthe.

THE drug lulled its patients into a repose of forgetfulness and warmth whenever thoughts about the Event arose. For a while, it appeared as though the Department had gained total control over this whole affair of the psyche, but alas, there were some of us who were unaffected by the Nepenthe… we were labelled Sanguinaires.

EVERY public and private institution was legally obligated to administer psychological tests and determine who was afflicted by this post-Event neurosis, otherwise known as the Sanguinaire condition. Once diagnosed, a Sanguinaire began the process of "Rectification" – and this is how Cooter and I ended up in the same room together.

NOW allow me to go back to Cooter and the events of that evening… I didn't know if I wanted to keep going on about the Event, especially in public.

I said to him, “Let’s be a little cautious. You never know who’s listening.”

“IN a joint as lavish as this, I don’t think we have anything to fear,” Cooter said and then gestured towards one of the sordid-looking bar fiends who was drooling into his glass. I marveled at this harmless wretch and felt my apprehensions get pushed aside. We proceeded to order many a round of whiskey and achieved an amicable level of staggering stupor.

AS our conversation began to ring louder, Cooter looked around and said, “Well then, sailor, since you’re sooo worried ’bout where we’re speak’n, I say we down these pints and scatter on outta here. I got a bottle of whiskey that longs to be drank; care thee, traveller, to venture back to my place?”

I replied giddily, “If your place is any more alluring than our current haven, I’ll have to decline. I wouldn’t be able to handle civility or cleanliness at a time as precious as this.”

COOTER retorted, “Worry not, kind sir, this captain’s quarters are the furthest thing from an actual home.”

WE both laughed and soon departed. I felt like I had joined forces with Captain Ahab.

CALL me Laertes…

FOUR
THE DEBAUCH

RAIN AT OUTDOOR PARTIES
COFFEE STAINS ON TIES
LAND MINES

MOST people fail to grasp the contagion of booze. They only see its consequences and can't for the life of them comprehend how a man can sacrifice his only chance at stability for a momentary bout of self-immolation. I believe most people seek refuge in the bottle as a last-ditch attempt at avoiding madness. Me? I think if life affords even the slightest hope of immortality, then it is in the pawning of one's soul for Bacchic revelry and an alcohol-induced delirium…

COOTER had found this slimy cauldron covered in ash-butted filth that was situated right beside the back alleyway door of the bar we'd just vacated. It acted as the hearth around which all the crooked-eyed bar fiends would gather and commiserate, smoking idly and exchanging tips on what kind of roofies worked best on their favourite waitresses. Cooter thought of himself as a man of class and distinction, and so he made the effort to toss his butt out in the designated rusty tin bowl. Unfortunately, he managed to hit a car parked nearby. The cigarette was blown over by a passing wind, and before we knew it we saw the car's six-foot owner and his sidekick muscle their way in our direction.

"YO, why you fucking ashin' dat shit on my car, yo?" asked one of the meatheads.

I attempted to make a drunken overture to the fellow by assuming responsibility for the imaginary damages. "We didn't mean to flick anything at your car… the wind must've blown it over. I am very sorry." Cooter just stood there indifferent and amused, taking no ownership for what he'd done and offering little in the way of support to me.

THE pale, bloated creature replied, "I don't fucking care, yo, you're gonna break my car with that shit!" His gangly mope of a companion grunted behind him in an apish show of support.

"HOW? It's just a fucking cigarette. Nothing's broken; everything is fine. I apologize regardless, but really there's no point in fighting over this. If you look for a problem, you can always find one, but let's stop looking and move on, fellas. Whaddya say?"

THE ghoulish sidekick wasn't interested in my humanitarian efforts. "Nah, yo, I heard you fucks talking shit at the bar. Looking down on Bonnie. Givin' her a tough time and shit, asking fer yer fancy-ass hipster beers, yo. She works hard fer her money and supports two kids, it ain't easy, bud, so drink yer imports and talk your homo talk elsewhere."

THE Neanderthal took over, "Ye yo, trying to act better than us, you guys are a bunch'a goofs talk'n kife all nite. Faggots, eh, Korey!" The imp assented, seething all the while. "No one cares 'bout yer big words, and we don't want ya comin' round here, yo. I don't wanna listen to you little bitches whining 'bout bullshit… fucking faggots!

"YA, yo!!!" snarled the sidekick demon. "Fags!"

SO we had finally ascertained the real reason for their rage. I looked to Cooter, signaling him to start walking, but right as I turned my head back I was socked in the kisser. Disoriented for a moment, I tried to regain composure whilst returning blows. Fumbling, falling and flailing, we both smashed into fences and collided with chairs. Bottles flew past my head and smashed all around us. At one point the demon I was wrestling with threw me across a patio table. I literally slid over it, leaving overturned, half-filled pint glasses in my wake, dispersing the crowd who had been sitting around them.

I struggled to find Cooter, who had tucked himself into the gathering crowd. I figured he was the one chucking the bottles which appeared to be raining from the sky just behind the mob. Then, out of nowhere, Cooter ran up and smashed a chair over the head of the second ghoul. He then grabbed a pipe he'd spotted beside a beat-up radiator and busted the window of the goon's car. The whole scene reminded me of some kind of spaghetti western bar fight from one of those ol' John Ford flicks, rife with banjos playing as flying pieces of splintered wood, furniture and bottles clashed and crashed in the dust… in a way I felt honoured to have played a part on one of those classic cinematic stages.

I heard Cooter scream, "I'll smash your fucking head, get over here!" The two heathens slithered off, licking their wounds while whimpering under their breath about the now very real damages to their car. It was glorious. Cooter tossed the pipe at the second goon in a marvelous boomerang-type fashion, hitting him deftly in the ribs, and we watched smugly as the oaf keeled over, cowering and weeping with his six-foot crony. Someone watching warned us that they were calling the police. The rest were just recording it all on their phones and taking very little in.

COOTER was beaming with pride. "Job well done, Laertes! But wow, did you ever get licked! Come on, let's hurry on back to my place. If Ezri's there, she'll stitch that shiner right up for ya! Hot damn!"

WE heard police sirens in the distance and scattered off into a network of back alleys. Just as I started to really feel the damage that had been inflicted upon my poor face, we arrived at Cooter's apartment in the ass-end of East York. We paraded in with gusto, only to find splintered fragments of a relationship once valued staring back at us in the form of a despairing lover. The living room looked like a recently excavated dungeon. It was a squalid place laced with perpetual neglect, and one felt that it had worked hard to earn its glum and morose ambience. I couldn't complain, though; I was just a wounded soldier, the most recent in what I'm sure was a long line of sorry cases to have staggered through these doors under exactly these circumstances.

"AH, you're awake, my lady!?" Cooter inquired in a regal tone, fancying himself charming.

"I am," the freckled orchid replied, but not with the same baroque pungency...

"WELL then, get the whisky out. We have a visitor! He needs medical attention!"

THE tainted girl replied with mild scorn, "So you caught another stray. I see he's got a bump on his chin. What's this one's name? I can't keep up with your sidewalk cronies."

"THE name's Larteifucsmghu..." I interrupted – half kidding, half just in the bag.

SHE rolled her eyes annoyingly and replied, "Excuse me?"

ORGANIZING my thoughts drunkenly, I pitched her one of my backward points of view. "Well, it's not like you're gonna remember my name anyways, so I was thinking it'd be more fitting to gargle out a sound that represents me best."

SHE laughed a bit and responded, "Well, isn't that a stupidly unique answer. If you spoke with more brains and a lot less liquor, I might even say you were interesting." She looked keen and amused and, after this playful reprimand, she continued, "Wow, somebody really took a liking to you with that shiner. Come here and let me tend to that wound."

I stuttered a response in an effort to validate her suspicions about my character: "Yeah, we had a scuffle outside the bar... I am a bit disoriented, so if I say something stupid, just chalk it up to that."

THE girl replied, "Don't try to justify your idiotic entrance. You thought you were being clever and cool, but instead you sounded retarded. Now what say you tell me your name, for reals, because believe it or not, it does matter."

"LAERTES..." I pouted, knowing our fun was at its end and, surprisingly, finding myself wounded both physically and egotistically.

SHE laughed a bit and replied, "That's better. My name is Ezri – now hold still!"

COOTER barked something in the background as he searched for his rumoured libations. "Grand, just grand, I'm glad you guys met... now how'd we wander so far astray, where's the booze at, eh – Ezri? I demand to know at once! You always lose everything!" His companion just scowled at him. She fetched a Band-Aid and fixed me up right and good. After which she stared with barely repressed rage at Cooter.

EZRI was a frail assemblage of symmetrical proportions. As a whole she was an unexpected beam of radiance blessing her comrade's sullen trench. I'd garnish on some ornate explanation of her Scandinavian blonde hair, pale freckled skin and crystal blue eyes, but that would be fruitless; real beauty doesn't need a Shakespearean sonnet, and besides, I'm lazy and drunk.

COOTER and I started in on what we felt were the important matters of our times, spouting out our respective philosophical certainties. In reality we were just two idiots participating in a Homeric contest to spittle more saliva with each successive point: the only effective means by which to determine the victor.

AFTER a while we grew tired of this and began singing old commercial jingles instead. I love the little jingles. They distract me from this generation's cultural bankruptcy. Their catchy little melodies are infinitely more fun than the other mainstream musical options available, most of which emanate from the fraudulent "gangsters" of Forest Hill. Oh, how I hate them.

AFTER several hours of lubricated discourse, Ezri ventured the following: "So, Mr. Larguubignk… how did you come upon this dashing lover of mine… was it before the fight, or did you guys meet because of that?"

I slurred a soggy answer, "Well... your sir here offered me a night of ballyhoo. The troublesome part afterwards was quite unintended."

SHE chuckled and continued, "That still doesn't explain how you guys met."

COOTER gave me a consternated glance before I replied, "Oh, haha... through the meetings, I think? Yeah, that's it!"

I felt dethroned by her reaction to these words. "So you're a Sanguinaire too, eh? I figured that when you first opened that clipped mouth of yours. If there's one thing I can always count on with you bozos, it's your odd way of throwing muddled mumbo jumbo into everything you say and getting beat up for it. You guys are always trying to make a point of being serious. I don't see why you try so hard. I know the medication hits you differently, but it must do something… I always see Cooter and his friends snorting it."

MY new chum looked offended and barked at his mate, "They don't affect us the way you think, stupid. You know that already!"

STARTLED, she replied, "Regardless, I don't know why you bother. You never agree on anything and you make everyone around you feel bad. You just go on about the same tired subjects: the universe, death, God… and you never make any progress.

"WHY can't you just mellow out and leave it? You're not gonna change anything by going on like this… all night you two've been at it, and look where it's got you!

"LAERTES, you have no idea how difficult it is to deal with. I get that this stuff matters to him, but it makes him so cold and emotionally distant. He's empty when it comes to living or being in love. The only passion or excitement I can hope for is a wild outburst at the world's problems, and if he's not off on one of those tangents, he's drowning himself in drugs and alcohol or fighting in parking lots with partners in crime like you!"

COOTER looked at me with a grin and said, "For the record, we fought honourably." He smirked and nodded as if to say, "We showed her," and then continued, "And they're prescribed, the drugs."

"I don't care! They're still not good for you, and what about the drinking…?" Ezri put him in his place for the moment and continued, "I'm not stupid. I get the appeal of these ideas. For a while there, I thought I might be a Sanguinaire too, which maybe helps me to tolerate this mess of a relationship. But you don't want to share any of it. Not really. That's the problem with you guys: you all think you're the only ones that have these ideas or feel depressed about the world. What you don't get is that we all feel the same way; we just act on it differently.

HELL, it's just that you never stop, and I don't get where you find the energy to waste, especially when you offer so little toward everything and everyone else that should matter to you… You think I want to have a future with a man who believes he is the only one responsible for determining it? It's madness."

EZRI gave a nervous little laugh and then resumed in a serious tone, "And you all have this attitude about life, it's like an optimistic nihilism or something… I don't know, it doesn't work…"

REDIRECTING her diatribe toward me, she continued, "You talk a bit more flowery than Cooter, but he gets wordy too. It's good to see him talk to you, though. I often see him with the worst kind of people. I keep telling him to spend time with cultured people, educated people… He loves to lower himself by carousing with these scummy types. What do you think you gain from these shitheads?"

COOTER answered sarcastically, "Beats spending time with you… haha."

"FUNNY – see how he talks to me? He hangs out with 'them' because he thinks they're honest with themselves, which apparently means more to him than if they actually cared about him, like I do. I've given up trying to satisfy him in any way other than the bed. At least there we know what to expect from each other," Ezri finished, huffing in frustration and grief.

THE offended party of our gathering then reproached his woman, "Now you listen here, lady! Why must you bother my friends with your silly questions?"

EZRI couldn't stand it anymore. "If you call me little lady, girl or woman one more fucking time, I'll rip your balls off!"

IF couples can be said to have achieved anything in their endeavours to strain the pulp out of failed promises and vain attempts at love, it is to be found in the science of knowing exactly how to piss each other off. Cooter and his missus had their doctorates in this particular discipline.

"I'M not kidding, ya know!" she screamed. "I'll leave you! You're impossible to live with… or even to sleep with lately, if you really wanna get into it. Maybe that's it, maybe that's why you like to have these defectives as friends! You get more pleasure from them than you do me. Maybe you should go to bed with them. Maybe you could get it up for once!"

COOTER was in the thick of it – I could see the trouble gathering on his brow. Then his face cleared, and with an obvious look of derision in his drooping eye, he turned to me and asked, "Laertes, what do you say? Wanna be my lover?"

I laughed sincerely, cherishing every moment. "I don't know if being too drunk is holding me back or making me want to… hahaha." Ezri had misrepresented the failings of a Sanguinaire lover. It wasn't a secret that Sanguinaires couldn't get it up… but the homosexual implications were way off. We tended more towards the asexual side – which is why it surprised me that Cooter was even in a relationship.

"HAHAHAHA... you're just grand, Laertes, just grand," he said.

EZRI threw down something from the nearby shelf and screamed, "You don't even know this guy! I'm going to bed. I'm putting my pussy in a vault. I hope your little pecker feels guilty about all the assholes it's paid a visit to!"

EZRI bolted. What did I care, though? All I knew was that I was very drunk (and even knowing that was hard, given how drunk I was). More than anything, and despite how the evening had concluded, I was pleased that I had found someone who intended to drown what remained of his waking mind with as much dedication as I did. There is no bond stronger than the one that links two alcoholics together. It's every drunk's dream to find that special someone out there who can keep up... Truth be told, I had no time to waste with anyone else, and so began my relationship with Cooter.

Five

Remy's Ham

When you think soreness is temporary but it isn't
Family-owned stores in rapidly gentrifying areas
Obligatory patience

I awoke the next morning to the clanking and thuds of two cackling characters hacking darts and passing a bottle back and forth. After realizing that my phone was dead, I frantically looked for anything that might resemble a clock. I staggered to my feet and squinted my eyes, trying to determine where I was, which layer of hell I was in. I only remembered crossing the river Styx…

"HOW you doing, sailor? Hell of a night, eh?" said the barely recognizable voice from my recent past.

I responded in befuddlement, "Who's this guy?" gesturing toward the strange new face to Cooter's left as he nipped a swig of whiskey. A more important question soon followed. "Is there booze left from last night?"

"THERE sure is… and a fine Irish batch it be, hahahaha!" Cooter continued, "This here is my old pal, Remy. I can never sleep more than a few hours, so I shot him a text in the wee hours of dawn's ass crack, and what do you know, insomnia must be as insidious as any old venereal disease, 'cause the little scamp was up!" He coughed out a self-amused laugh.

THE stranger shouted, "Yo bud! How ya doin? GAAAAAK," He made this putrid gagging/coughing kind of sound after his greeting that resembled the dying gurgle of a road-killed rodent gargling on the leftovers of garbage still trapped in its crushed esophagus.

HE stood before me, this street urchin, beaming a big grin. He wore these tattered, baggy, gangster-ish jeans that were in a criminal state of neglect and a shirt that resisted any and all attempts to be tucked into his beltless pants. The teeth he still had were yellowish from years of smoking and the left front one was missing.

REMY was 'round 20 and looked like an accursed son from one of D.H. Lawrence's beloved coal mines. The kid was skeletal and prepubescent in appearance, but not entirely unattractive. If his hair and face weren't soaked in the soot and grease of street-carousing homelessness, you might even say he was cute.

REMY carried between his arms what looked like a rolled-up piece of ham. Hanging off the fishnet and keeping the ham together was a dangling little tag that said 'Murphy's Meats'. I didn't know what was more fucked up, the fact that I was in this dingy region of the underworld with some religious-psycho Sanguinaire, or that Murphy's produce was now at large and nestled in some street kid's armpit.

DISTRAUGHT by this surplus of compounding absurdity, I was forced to ask, "What's with the ham? Really, man… ham…?"

THE street kid smiled and replied, "Oh… I stole it," and he said it with a degree of pride which I have yet to find paralleled.

HE explained further, "I started this new butcher gig, and hey, I figured it's meat… if you're gonna make me work with it, then I better get a bite!" He spoke with a rat-like whip of the tongue that reminded me of the irritable whine of a cassette on fast-forward.

AMUSED, I replied, "So you steal from your employers on your first week. You don't waste any time, do you?"

"NOT me, bud," he said, giving off a radioactively vile grin. "You gotta take whatever you can get, bud! My pal Chucky boosts meats all the time from the Sunshine Tavern over on Dawes and Danforth, haha! One time I bought peanut butter from good ol' Chuck, straight outta the plastic grocery bag. I woulda' swiped the lamb too, but I ran outta shekels… If you can get it cheap, why not, yo?"

COOTER couldn't resist joining the conversation: "I was there for that. This slime bucket came in peddling lamb chops and peanut butter. I wouldn't jump at the meat, but the peanut butter was dandy." He said this in a wise tone, a true master of Danforth street bartering.

HIS friend then rejoined, "Anyways... I love workin' in a butcher shop as one of my many choice side gigs – that and removing asbestos in my bud's pickup truck."

HE rambled on, "Now the boss from my other gig loves me, cuz he knows I'm a real man, guess it's cuz I'm butcherin' meat, there ain't nothing like dicin' flesh that brings boys together, hahahahah! GAAAK! I don't get it, bud, but hey, I don't have to clean shitty toilets as a side duty no more cuz I've become a man. They got me on entrails duty!"

REMY'S appalling tale of blood, ham, theft and toilets had an endearing effect on me. I thought to myself, what other kind of conversation could be better tailored to this moment?

IT then dawned on me that my life needed some serious re-evaluation. And with that instant of well-overdue introspection came the remembrance that I had a few things I needed to do that afternoon. I teetered to my feet and asked the madmen what time it was.

COOTER replied, "Time? Who gives a fuck about time anymore… the only time that matters now is how much of it you got left…"

I was taken aback but responded promptly and honestly, "I guess… Well, I'll be kicking around for a little while longer. My dead end isn't so bad… cardiac arrest in my fifties. What about you, Cooter?"

COOTER blurted a violent reply, "Why the fuck do you care? There's no rhyme or reason behind any of it, according to you …"

BEFORE I could answer him, Remy yelped, "I'm gonna get hit by a car! GAAAAK!" And after almost hacking up a lung, he took another swig from Cooter's bottle.

I didn't want to champion another polemic and just commented casually, "You see, Cooter, Remy enjoyed sharing his death with us. You shouldn't get so sore, but I get it… it's early. I think I'll be on my way."

I started making a painful attempt to retrace last night's drunken footsteps and find my things. I waddled slowly and eventually found my keys in a swampy ashtray. I chose to risk the frothing diseases coagulating in that receptacle of filth and reached my hand in.

JUST as I was making my final farewells, we heard a knock at the fire escape window. In popped a familiar face that had spoken at last night's meeting. I'd seen him around enough times but had always avoided any meaningful contact that would have interfered with my general rule of hating people.

THIS morose character exuded a distraught and downtrodden temperament and exhaled resignation with every breath. I instantly felt there was something seriously wrong with him. He was anemic, boney and gaunt. He looked like he had barely survived some sort of plague. The oily black pores of his skin were complimented by these rotting fish eyes with a yellowish hue; I wish I could say there was even a hint of life behind them.

REGARDLESS, Cooter seemed to be excited by the guy's arrival and greeted his friend as he drunkenly maneuvered over to open the window. "If it isn't my mate Darius. What tearful tale of life's troubles are ya gonna lay upon us today?"

DARIUS awkwardly tried to squeeze himself through the tight opening and began, "Hi. Thought I'd just grab a gram of Nep. Didn't mean to interrupt your little shindig, guys."

REMY'S roach-like senses had detected that fresh trash was being dumped on the refuse pile, and he scuttled frantically towards Darius, hoping to exploit the filthy process. "I got $18.25… can I pitch in on that? Cooter won't sell anything less than a gram. Please, bud!!! GAAAK."

JUST to clarify, Nepenthe was accessible with a prescription, but ever since the Department realized it wasn't affecting us in the way they'd intended, they had cancelled most of our official means of accessing the drug. I often find it's the legal drugs that are most difficult to come by. Regardless, a lot of Sanguinaires would mislead their Rectification leaders into thinking that the Nepenthe was helping, and those who couldn't just knew somebody on the inside. Cooter was clearly one of these proud dealers.

UNFAZED, the sullen character at the window just stared blankly through Remy and responded, "I really don't care anymore. You can pitch, just as long as I still have enough to get my groove on."

THE greatest pleasure for an addict is in scoring when he thought he wasn't going to get any. This was evidenced by Remy's pure and uncontrollable jubilation. They bought their batch from Cooter and sat down on the couch with a gaiety with which not even the laughter of children could compare or compete.

DARIUS snorted a line and turned to me. "You were at last night's meeting, weren't you?"

"I was. I'm Laertes."

HE continued, "Yea, I've heard you go at it with Ronald a couple times. You kinda remind me of Cooter. I'm sure you've noticed he's the same way. It's what I like about him."

I was not flattered by this comparison and answered with as much sarcastic disdain as I could muster. "I see... so you're attracted to fools who can't keep their mouths shut?"

DARIUS made an attempt to laugh but it sounded more like a puff of dry smoke. "Yeah, I guess. I envy you guys your anger. Once you run out of that, it's hard to get it back. You just stop fighting at some point. The Department doesn't get that... sooner or later everyone goes numb to everything. I'm not quite there yet, but with any luck I'll get there soon."

COOTER interjected, "Not talkin' about that dark day around the corner will do that. I keep tellin' ya, just keep talking. One day you might just talk your way outta your own execution!"

DARIUS replied, "I do talk. Mostly with my dad, you know..."

COOTER jumped in, "Tell Laertes 'bout it, bucko, maybe he'd be interested. You know where I stand on it. Tell'm 'bout your brave an' loving father..."

DARIUS sighed then shifted his glassy-eyed stare to me. His skeletal frame was becoming animated, so I figured what was coming next must be important. "My dad lectures at the University of Toronto. He's trying to help us Sanguinaires with the Event. He's trying to push therapy over meds as the go-to method of treatment. You see, he's got a background in medical science, used to work close with the Department, but he's moved beyond that now. He's all about talking openly, not just with each other at the meetings. He wants our whole society to get back into the conversation. You should see his face light up when a personality type like you drops into his classroom and joins in the discussion..."

COOTER snorted derisively. "I still say he's talkin' shit. He only wants to 'listen' so that he can seem controversial and have something racy to say in front of his colleagues. 'Look how the other half lives. Aren't I so fucking cultured and open-minded.' Hogwash! That's how these guys work. It's just virtue mongering at its finest, and I don't give a damn that he's your pa either. Fuck anyone who clears that much money a year in the name of 'healing and helping the afflicted to mend their wounds!' They think they control everyone because people toss 'em a 'sir' now and then. If ya took away their little titles they'd just stand still; they'd freeze and stammer, blubbering idiots with a single focus and a real sorry track record when it comes to any real action. All he's gonna do is piss in intellectual circles, and I don't want to smell his credentials!"

I, like Cooter, find it difficult to trust that smooth and unassailable class of elevated observers that make up the academic elite, a group which Darius's father apparently fell right smack in the middle of. They're the anthropologists who will fiercely defend the groups of indigenous peoples they've just finished exploiting.

I decided to do a little fishing. "I'd imagine your father would have some difficulty mentioning the Event in his lectures, though? I thought the Department was against spreading views that could potentially worsen our 'fragile mental condition'? Surely it's a very serious charge to misguide the youth these days."

DARIUS'S limp body with its slouchy centre slowly began to change. I could see a jitter rising up in him... could it possibly be an emerging posture? It was a sketched-out twitch, accompanied by a paranoiac gander peering out from the half-sealed trashcans that were his homeless eyes. His ugly excitement suggested I had said something that pleased him.

DARIUS pleaded, "He needs us, guys... Cooter, man, you don't understand, your attitude is what fucks everything up. You keep talking about action, but what're you doing? Laertes, right? You seem reasonable. I know you're not happy with the Department, all the useless drugs, all this bullshit! Please, come down to one of his lectures with me and talk to him. He barely has time for me these days... but I'm sure if I brought a new face with me, he'd make an exception..."

I pondered for an instant, I hadn't graduated all that long ago, and I still had a lingering connection to the ol' institute of higher learning, and so I said, "I went there, ya know. What's your old man's name?"

DARIUS replied solicitously, "Bakhshi, Professor Bakhshi... it's Persian if you're wondering. He's the one that looks like the former Shah of Iran."

LAUGHING a bit, I replied, "I can't say I know him. I'd remember the Shah. Then again, my courses were strictly on the arts side of the old arts and science divide... To tell you the truth, I wouldn't mind checking out my old stomping grounds, regardless of any loftier revolutionary-type aim."

DARIUS said, "He's teaching later this afternoon. Take my number, shoot me a text and we'll meet up!" He directed the invitation exclusively to me, knowing that Cooter would be unsupportive and uninterested.

I thought about what I was committing myself to and remembered that I had some other things to do that day.

I bid the room a farewell address then thought to ask Cooter if I could have his number too.

COOTER guzzled the last morsel of whiskey in a panic and blinked back at me with flustered eyes. "Just knock at the window, man, everyone does. Come back when you're done with Darius. I mean, you don't have to, but you should, man... If not, don't forget I'm at the meetings Mondays and Thursdays. Or else you can catch me at work. I tend bar over at The Eastern. Oh, and watch out for the crackheads downstairs. They like to sleep on the stoop. Usually I squeeze a foghorn through the mail slot to wake them up and get them moving. You can borrow it if you want?"

LAUGHING again, I replied, "Splendid... no, I think I'll be

fine. Anyways, it was a pleasure meeting you all, and please tell Ezri it was nice meeting her too. Toodles!"

I felt that each of them was digging their talons deep into me. I couldn't shake the feeling that there had been something off about Cooter that morning… he'd seemed needy, which didn't jive with the rest of his character. Both he and Darius had some kinda template for me to fill. It's awful when you meet someone and realize that they've already crafted a role for you. The two of them had an aim… or maybe they were just lonely. Well, at least if I didn't work out, they'd always have their loveable Remy to fawn over.

I scampered for the door and broke out into the streets. Crackheads to the right of me, junkies to the left … on through the alleyway I charged. Oh, half a league, half a league I darted, out of the valley of lifelessness, and emerged just as a streetcar came to whisk me away…

Six

Walking Down Memory Lane

People who have their whole lives ahead of them
Secretly enjoying funerals
Conditional love

DARIUS and I met up that afternoon in order to fulfill our hungover promise. We blustered our way into a tightly congested lab-type classroom, pulsating with the flow of youthful 'enlightenment'. I heaved a whiskey salute as I fell into my tiny seat: disheveled, disheartened and still a bit drunk...

AS I slouched into the chair, I bequeathed a contemptuous sneer upon all the little classroom keeners.

WE had come in a little later than the rest of them and tried to be as inconspicuous as possible. Being amongst "them" was like entering a Borg cube. I felt sure they couldn't see much beyond their collective hive mind of social media, and this allowed us to pass through undetected.

I was happy to keep quiet in the back. Half my mind was envisioning the range of intoxicants that would accompany the end of this lecture; the other half was trying to gauge the odds of the professor actually bringing up the Event in an academic setting. If he did… well, that meant that change might very well be on the horizon. Maybe they were finally coming to terms with the fact that some people really did care about dying and couldn't just pretend to go on as if they didn't. It seemed too good to be true.

COULD a priest of science, garbed in bureaucratic pragmatism, really be selling out his religion of rationality? Could he really do it under the all-seeing eye of the Department? I had to learn the guy's angle. I had to figure out why Darius was so sure of this pretend revolution. It's cute when people try to make a difference, but what struck me most in his particular case was that Darius didn't seem like a passionate person. So why the farce? And why did he need to have me there?

UNLIKE most Sanguinaires, I've never felt that instant connection with my fellow disenfranchised, nor have I felt inclined to fraternize with them about my views and values, or lack thereof. My mortal burden isn't made any easier by the knowledge that others are sharing it with me. In fact, I hate people who take comfort in knowing that someone else shares their miserable disorder or disease.

ANXIETY started to creep over me, and I gripped the little desk as tight as I could to try and steady myself. I wanted so badly for the sickly sweet strangeness of this episode to be over so that I could once again take refuge in the bosom of the bottle. But I had a sad little sidekick now, and he wouldn't partake in my pints unless I first became a fellow audience member to his father's spectacular spewing…

I found myself pondering how it was that I kept getting caught up in these slithery cosmic collisions and the troublesome episodes that ensued… I needed to slow down… and yet there was always another adventure of this sort waiting in the wings… Ok, back to the classroom. I'll try to stop veering off.

PROFESSOR Bakhshi did indeed look like the Shah, but he carried with him an aura of patsy American assuredness, very different from the usual stiff-neck attitudes I was used to encountering in these settings. He began to speak, and there was a frank affability to him that complimented his bushy grey eyebrows and grey sideburns.

I was curious to see how long he could remain 'objective', "calm" and "neutral" about the subject at hand. It seemed he'd perfected a manner that would prevent his being discovered as an agitator. As I've said, there was nothing illegal about discussing the Event... it was just unwise if you valued your job, identity and livelihood.

PROFESSOR Bakhshi began the lecture with a purely historical angle that confused the fuck out of me... In a professional and coherent fashion, the Shah managed to summarize the history of a sage named Solon. Solon, the Shah explained, was once purported to be the wisest man in Athens, and because of this, his opinion was sought after by a wealthy king of ancient times named Croesus.

I'LL put it in an even tighter nutshell than old Bakhshi did: Croesus asks Solon whether he, the king, is the happiest man alive. Solon is expected to answer in the affirmative because Croesus possesses exorbitant wealth and power. Instead, Solon tells the king that no one can know if he is the happiest man alive until after he has died.

PROFESSOR Bakhshi concluded thusly: "You can only ever know a man's worth posthumously. The bulk of life's import, meaning and subsequent happiness can only be validated once you have lived your whole life right to its end. From this premise, class, I'd like you to ask yourselves: would Croesus have been better off if he had known exactly when and how he was going to die? What if he could have taken a pill that guaranteed he would make certain choices, adopt certain means of behaviour? Could he then have told the wise Solon, 'No, I am indeed the happiest man alive, as no part of my life remains unknown to me'? And should anyone have this kind of self-certainty? I'd like us to perch for a moment on this cornerstone of ethics, fate, faith and science."

ONE of the students in the front row was uncomfortable and asked: "Wouldn't that be a Sanguinaire way of looking at the question, sir? They always try to talk about death and fate and stuff. They all think there's something special about what they've seen in their visions. Isn't it safer to avoid this kind of thinking altogether?"

THE professor countered calmly, "Surely there is no danger in engaging these subjects when you are able to think like you and I, like healthy people. It is the unhealthy way in which those mentally afflicted souls approach these subjects that causes harm, not the subjects themselves. Do we really think that every time someone mentions mortality or fate, they are somehow affirming the Sanguinaire way of looking at things? Or, put another way, is a subject wrong as a whole just because it can be appropriated to a mistaken point of view?"

THE flustered young man replied, "I'm sorry again, but all of this is just coming off like the same kind of nonsense I hear them say. Can't we just be objective here? That stuff is messed up and it's not nice to think about."

THE professor replied quickly and with a shocking lack of caution, "Well, what is it that they say? And why does it hurt you so much that they believe in something you think is wrong?"

THE student whined and writhed in his chair, "I don't *think* they're wrong. I *know* for certain they're wrong. It's not just me – everyone agrees, except them, and that's only because their brains can't accept reality, medication or therapy. I have a cousin who's afflicted and I have to watch her struggle through life, getting hooked on drug after drug. She's had loads of failed relationships and just stews on her own doing nothing because her vision is more important to her than work, family or anything else. No way she's any freer than someone undergoing Rectification therapy. Besides, even if it wasn't wrong, who the heck would want to live that way?"

THE professor's tone was soothing now. "I understand. I'm sorry for you and for your cousin. And no one is trying to discredit the pain and suffering this condition brings to Sanguinaires and to everyone around them. But what I'm trying to ask is why it offends you to merely hear an idea like fate or prophecy brought up? Even within the safe and distant context of an ancient Greek myth? Don't we empower the Sanguinaire point of view more by treating these subjects as catastrophic and destructive things? Wouldn't it discredit the importance they place on these issues if we were able to discuss them casually? Academically? Can't you –"

HE was interrupted mid-sentence. "No! No one should ever say there's something 'behind' anything else, especially not the *Event*. No one should think or talk about anything like this. It's disgusting. This isn't the kind of stuff I'm paying thousands in OSAP to learn, and I won't be lumped into whatever messed-up position you're arguing on their behalf, Mr. Bakhshi!"

I saw the recognition of defeat as it passed across Professor Bakhshi's face. He had clearly become an expert in the art of backpeddling. "Believe it or not, you and I are in perfect agreement, Kyle, when it comes to the subjects that matter. I know I express my views strangely sometimes, which can lead to misunderstandings, and for that I apologize. As you know, I am a scientist, and perhaps part of me just wanted to test how you would all react to challenging material. But in this case, I guess I took it too far. The whole business interests me purely as an academic curiosity, something in line with

Jung or Freud. But your point is well made and well taken. We will stay on surer scientific footing for the remainder of the hour…"

AND by God, if the disappointing old bastard didn't remain mind-numbingly true to his word. I drifted off for most of it, and when I was later roused into being again by the welcome announcement that time was up, I found I'd been staring intently at a pimple on the neck of the guy in front of me. Bakhshi waved for us to come up to the front as the gaggle of student furies scattered.

LOOKING down at his son as if he were standing on a stage, the professor spoke thusly, "You're not supposed to barge in here like this. It's not like all the other halfway homes you spend most of your time in. My job is difficult enough as it is. What if it had lined up with the Rectification monitor's checkup? I could get in serious trouble for having you here. You should know better."

DARIUS sulked submissively and replied, "I wanted you to meet someone, Dad. I just thought you had some views in common. I figured it'd be good for him to hear your perspective and thought you'd be happy to meet him too."

THE Shah look-alike was somewhat placated. "Well, fine, but I'd have appreciated some warning."

DARIUS muttered unintelligibly, "I thought… I just thought you wanted this… besides, he used to go here."

THE professor concluded his scolding: "Next time just bring him over to the house – that is, if you ever decide to come home."

BAKHSHI looked at me, and I could see he felt guilty for

flagrantly embarrassing his son. "Ahem. I apologize. I didn't mean to be so rude. What's your name, sir?"

"LAERTES."

THE professor mused, "Odd one that, classical Greek name, no?"

"YUP. My family ran out of current Greek names, so we had to get archeological to find one."

BAKHSHI laughed a bit and then replied, "I've got quite a penchant for the ancient Greeks myself, as you may have noticed. I can't help myself. I minored in the classics way back when, and I have to admit there's probably as much mythos as there is science in a third or so of my lectures."

I was eager to move the conversation forward. "Ya, I noticed that. It was fun to see you bring up taboo material in that class."

"MMM. 'Reducing Scientific Barriers.' That's the name of this course. We explore innovative solutions to some of science's biggest hurdles... Although I can't tell you how depressingly uncreative today's drugged-up youth are ... but the class lends itself to a 'visionary' place, and the school can't blame me quite so easily for the conversations that follow. I report every student's ideas and responses directly to the Department, and in return they let me continue with my research. It's a fair price to pay. You know, only three-quarters of the population is affected by medical treatment?"

IT seemed to me he'd changed the subject, so I asked him directly, "What exactly are you trying to accomplish with all of this?"

THE professor paused for a moment, then he answered me, "I want to create the right kind of conversation. Instead of flagellating ourselves over the fact that we care about the Event, I want to promote discussion about what that experience entails. I want everyone to talk about their visions openly and to figure out if that might ease the anguish without the need for harsh medication. It's no coincidence I threw out Carl Jung back there. He's almost always at the forefront of my mind. If I could find a way to prove that the Event was a moment of collective unconsciousness… but that drugs numb the mind, dull the senses. It's a nightmare for the scientific community. How is anyone to make any future discoveries or realizations if all our scientists are struggling to keep their neural synapses firing? It's too depressing to think about. Mind you, my way's not moving things along much faster…"

THE professor continued, "My biggest qualm with the D.P.W. is how hastily they drugged everyone. No one got the chance to realize the importance of what they were dealing with. And now it's too late to speculate significantly about the Event because the majority of people are already compromised. That's why I'm looking for Sanguinaires to involve in my own discussion groups."

DARIUS turned to me and said, "Think you might find it worthwhile, Laertes?"

FLUSTERED by all this talk of revolutions, collective unconsciousness and government conspiracies, I made the only appropriate response I could, "Sounds like a hoot! Well then, I have places to be and things to do." I wasn't nearly drunk enough for this late hour of the afternoon.

WITH that said, I left them to the torment of being alone with one other. I felt all out of sorts and only knew for certain that I was not going to be swinging by Professor Bakhshi's discussion group. What a waste of an afternoon to deal with existence in this way. Alas, we must all fraternize in the world of the living once in a while.

AS I walked down the hallway, I heard Darius mutter to his father, “I really came just to see you. We barely get to talk, even when I am home. I haven’t been sleeping… I can’t stop thinking about it.”

THE professor made an angry reply. “Have you been going to your meetings? I don’t want you taking those drugs, but I need you to be attending the meetings. I can’t have them identifying you as a truant. The last thing I need is the Department knowing I have an untreated Sanguinaire son. It would compromise my position even more. You know I’m trying, don’t you? I’m doing everything I can. Do you even care how your actions affect me? Does it ever occur to you?”

DARIUS responded, hurt, “This is my life; it’s not a fucking joke, Dad...”

“NO, this is *my* life’s work, and you’re ruining it.” And with that stinging remark, they had thankfully dropped out of earshot…

SevEn

Ouroboros (Ekansss!!!)

Sudden infant death syndrome
Being told that everything will be okay
Solutions that create more problems

A couple of weeks went by and, through great insistence on Cooter's part, he and I developed what I suppose could be referred to as a 'bond'. We frequented the same watering holes, before and after the meetings, and in this way we became ever closer. I gathered that he and Ezri had parted ways and wasted many a moment in picturing what must have been a terrifically torrid final farewell. Cooter seemed largely unaffected by his change in romantic status; I imagine the booze deserves most of the credit for that also.

ONE dreary day, at Cooter's request, I found myself at the entryway of the righteous establishment that had seen fit to employ my backward-thinking companion. I had never been there before, but right away I felt a sense of ease and comfort with the place. I was home.

BEFORE Cooter, I had known the unique pleasure of not hating myself quite as much as I hated others, and this had allowed me to remain solitary most of the time. I hadn't needed to bamboozle others into befriending me in order to rid myself of my lonesomeness. Methinks that all interactions should be an exchange of goods – you're only as good as what you barter, and the second you run out, fall short or have nothing left to say, I just don't see the point in maintaining the relationship.

BUT now I had a committed acquaintance... Truth be told, my exchanges with Cooter were starting to get a little boring. They were all predicated on the assumption that this was the best of all possible worlds, and that outlook can only stay fresh for so long. But this day I had tagged along in the hopes of finishing a debate we had gotten into briefly the night before, one that I took great interest in. You see, I had been dutifully contending that Smart Food couldn't be considered a real form of popcorn, a position against which my companion vehemently disagreed. I have long felt that the only sure way to win an argument is to have already had the whole thing out with yourself and danced victoriously amidst the ashes of your opposing self. I was especially prepared for this one.

SO here I was, at the tavern Cooter worked at, and to my surprise it was quite the dazzler. It possessed a sort of Chet Baker cool jazz charm... the kinda place where Billie Holiday might have softly hummed a solo long before her heroin days. The walls were all exposed brick, accented with enlarged photos featuring Toronto from the early '20s. There were ruby-red booths with duskily lit lanterns hanging over each one. I couldn't see how a deadbeat like Cooter had been embraced by a hub of such class and character; nonetheless, I relished the fact that I had an intro.

THE place had a real jive beat to it. They specialized in serving up Sazeracs, Negronis and Old Fashioneds, which you could see being flung around, fast and loose. It was as if we were at an underground ball in the prohibition era, romping its way into the 21st century. And Cooter was the main event, the veteran juggler of this hodgepodge timescape of a rattling hullabaloo.

I saw him right as I came in, looking sharp and menacing. His bartending manner was as surly as they come, but I think that's an important part of the whole mystique bartenders try to create to disguise the fact that they're just glorified babysitters for hopeless drunken patrons. He stood behind the bar wearing a red vest and a crooked black tie, and it looked like the saloon was just an extension of his old soul. What a soul it was. You could feel it pulsating out of every brassy Boston shaker, up and down the velvet-lined seats and copper leggings of each bar stool. With one hand placed on the wood of the bar and the other hand on his hip, Cooter was trumpeting tall tales to a gaggle of furies, each looking to snatch a dollar out of his fifty-cent fibs…

IT didn't matter what he said to them: he could steer his stories in any direction he pleased, he could take his hands clean off the wheel and let the wind guide his words. No matter what he said, it was met with the same swooning, dewy-eyed response from every lazy lout limping sadly over that bar. The man was a bard in every sense of the term, and he found a way of keeping the roll fresh… his primary instrument of seduction was his shaker, a rumbling drum, playing out like one of Chick Webb's symphonies, with crashing ice cubes for cymbals. He rattled that metal tin with such voracious intent that the thing would freeze over, leaving a five-finger impression of his hot hand…

COOTER was a modern day outlaw. A charlatan who had found a way to pander cheap tricks and silly stories whose content mattered far less than their delivery. There was within him something quintessentially classic. He was the real McCoy of barkeeps, his sad but exciting life performed on a broken stage in front of languishing drunks that sometimes stood and sometimes tumbled. Always he was there as their entertainer, awaiting meagre pocket change which would hopefully amount to enough for him to get himself drunk once the rest had left.

HE saw me come in and gave me a menacing gaze, an even mixture of suspicion and excitement. He kept his eyes locked on me amidst his juggling. I realized then that this was often the case. These optical tangos were his stickups, and I lost parts of my manhood in each and every one. It was truly odd, especially because he emoted this real sense of aloofness towards everyone else. Even Darius and Remy got far less attention than I did.

AFTER losing yet another stare down, I approached the bar, dodging a few morons who stood stubbornly in the centre walkway. I hate it when people just stand in the middle of things, always with this toilsome look of bewilderment etched into their ugly mugs. Anyways… I overcame this great adversity and Cooter greeted me with laughter, having borne witness to my awkward maneuvering around the human pylons.

"AHOY, mate! You finally came by my joint… I didn't think you were gonna show. I'd like you to meet some of these upstanding fellas of mine. Well, you know Darius already..."

COOTER pointed to his friends as they grumbled hello and gave me a reluctant nod or two… These spiteful pirates hated me the same way a pathetic patron at a strip bar hates the new guy with the bulkier wallet for taking away the attention of his favourite stripper.

ASIDE from Cooter, Darius was the only one I knew, and I was relieved to see him. Darius looked a little tired, though. He was clearly disinterested in whatever the fuck Cooter was telling the gang. The kid was the only one kind enough to bless me with the honour of a handshake, and so I felt compelled to reciprocate by purchasing his next club soda and lime.

I gave the group a quick look over and immediately assumed they were Sanguinaires. Why else would they be hanging off the words of a flagrant grumbler obsessed with fate and freewill? Sure enough, the whole platoon turned out to be mentally afflicted misanthropes, pounding back brews, patiently awaiting the roll call of their respective meetings. The bar/restaurant's crowd in general looked like it consisted solely of half-life dregs meandering the plains of Elysium, hopelessly gazing over their menus with clueless, doomed expressions written on their faces. I was terrified.

I looked around and found a bit of solace in knowing that at least I belonged with these freaks at the bar. In a funny way, being a Sanguinaire made the human condition more tolerable, precisely because we were all fully aware of how terrible it was and didn't give a damn about trying to hide it. But that feeling wasn't enough to keep me there long, and after a few moments of awkwardly trying to find an entrance into an irrelevant conversation, I debated trying to leave.

SEEING Darius also struggle with the group, however, brought about a mutually assured sense of discomfort… a sense that it couldn't be worse for both of us. And then I became privy to some new information that really sealed the deal and ensured my continued presence, information that could have compelled me to remain in a concentration camp for an indefinite period of time after liberation. This information had to do with the bar's selection of draughts – they had cider. Oh, how I love my cider!

I soon had a pint of this lovely liquid bubbling merrily away in front of me, and I was just preparing to commit myself fully to Darius when I was accosted once more by Cooter's overbearing zeal. Again I sensed in him a frantic anxiety to keep me all to himself. Surely the fellow could tell there were others there who wanted his attention far more than I did.

I could see that the zest of his personality inexplicably drew people into a captivated sort of trance. They relished his vigour, I felt, rather than the real essence of his passionate personality. What I liked about him was his distaste for anything repressed or unauthentic. He was Reality incarnate, and it was painful to see that the others were simply amused by his angry forcefulness. I'm fucked if I know what he ever got from them in return, and I never cared enough to ask.

DESPITE his verve and his unrelenting didacticism, Cooter struck me as being a very sad person. I knew that even if he did feel that way, he'd never let on, and I was grateful to him for that. We both managed to respect not really getting to know the wounds and hurts of one another, and I think that's what I relished about the relationship. It's a lot nicer to be honest about not giving a shit than pretending to care about someone else's problems.

COOTER shouted over at me over the grunts and squeals of his swine-like fan base, "So how's it going, chap? Still hacking away at life's grand mystery? Been back to see Darius's pop at all? He's got all the answers, he does, or so says his PhD. These academics, eh, they all got revolutionary theses. Ask them to apply the things to real life and watch what a mess they make, eh, Darius?" he said this with a devilish grin.

I was bored of his constant posturing, his relentless self-promotion of a salt-of-the-earth-type intellect, his irate "all's ya need" bag of self-reliance and stalwart simplicity. He was your classic Bukowskian persona, pretending to lament formality and proper prose, and all the while capitalizing on the largest audience he could muster with the help of well-researched wit, a famous publishing house or a wealthy TV producer friend, all of which they purport to detest. These types seem to cower from the attention they claim to hate, and yet they always find themselves smack dab in the centre of it, profiting 'accidentally'.

IT'S the same thing with the beatniks, with their Kerouac Bedouin crutch. Jack's *Dharma* would have you believe that enlightenment can be found in a hooker's motel. Woody Allen wants everyone to think his only true "love" is for baseball and he could care less about psychoanalytic theory. "Who, me?" he asks. "I didn't mean to create a movie about human suffering; I just like watching the Nets."

I hate this counterfeit wisdom, marketed as a tainted but fashionable genius. The con artists who realize they can make more from imitations of original works and so never create original works of their own. The seedy salesmen who pitch their exegesis to a self-hating audience. These guys just stagger about, with this "clumsy" bravado and a self-entitled coolness, all the while pretending that they're clueless. They're going for Peter Falk's Columbo but they're missing the charm of his sad, crooked, one-eyed face... Give it up, man, there's nothing more overplayed than the common man card.

HAVING said this, Cooter and I probably still had more in common with each other than not. It was our approaches that differed. I had my own principles, and meeting Darius's dad didn't take anything away from them. Even if Bakhshi was full of shit it, I'd rather determine that for myself and not just assume it.

I asked Cooter, "So besides insulting anyone who has an education, what did you want to talk to me about?"

SLIGHTLY flustered, he stalled in his reply. "Hold up a sec! I gotta make this drink... who the fuck orders a Caesar at this time of night? It's the longest goddamn drink to make. I literally need to take out six things I already put away... Who orders this?!" I couldn't help but laugh.

DARIUS blurted out an awkward interruption. "So my dad mentioned the Department is coming up with a new form of treatment. I guess we're gonna hear about it at tonight's meeting. He's asked any of us who are interested to come back to our house when it's over and talk with him about it. I think he's trying to put something pretty big together, and he needs our help, as many of us as he can get – that means you too, Cooter..."

TO my surprise, Cooter's responding grunt sounded like a reluctant assent. At this point, we heard a loud holler from across the room. "Howdy!!!" We looked up and saw a gangly kid stumble through the swaying door. It was none other than our beloved and drunkenly virile Remy. He strode rakishly toward us. Cooter tossed down the dreaded drink he had been making, ignoring the waitress's pleas for him to finish, so that he could give Remy a proper salute.

"AHHH... Mr. Remy, how goes it?! What took ya so long?"

CLEARING his throat and/or swallowing whatever was still in there, Remy started right in: "The baby mamma's at it again, but I can't help it, ya know? I just love poking her, beached whale or no! But I can't stick around once she starts nagging me," he concluded jeeringly.

"HOW'S work?" baited Cooter.

"OH bud, do I have a story for YOU... Okay, you know creepy Rick, yo?" asked Remy.

COOTER smiled. "Yeah, but tell these guys too!"

REMY was more than pleased to spread the infection that was his life to anyone that would house the disease. "Hahaha, okay, okay... So guys, imagine that stereotypical trench-coat-wearing pedophile type that your folks warned you not to take candy from. Well, this is him, literally him, yo!

"BUD, so I was like working at this buffet over in Scarborough. It's like a trough for the sewer pigs of the city. So Rick's this old drunkard, yo, I mean he's always loaded, bud... You gotta understand the poor guy's wife died a ways back and his kids up and left him, so now he hangs out at the buffet literally giving candy to the staff, and they're always the perfect temperature... How's he do that?"

"ANYWAYZ, today he comes up to me and says, 'Hey there Remy, there's a personal matter I'd like to discuss with you, but we'll have to go to the washroom.'

"I says 'Ya, bud, sure thing there, Ricky.' How could I miss out on a once-in-a-lifetime chance like this!? GAAAAAAK!!!!!!!" We all laughed hard, Darius included.

HE continued, "So I go in there, giddy as a schoolgirl, and he reaches into his coat. I didn't know whether to expect a gun or a dick, but he pulls out this bag from the dollar store, and then he takes out some socks, yo. Bud, what the fuck? I was kinda disappointed, but then it kinda made a bit of sense. I guess not everyone who asks for a gathering in the pisser is gonna try to sell you drugs or fuck ya..." Remy sounded truly saddened by this last part.

"SO, after he takes out the bag, I says to him, I says, 'Thanks, Ricky, I'll be sure to put them on tomorrow for work,' just trying to get him going, bud... 'Oh, but that's not all,' he tells me, then he pulls out some underwear and says to me, 'Remy, I tried them on but shucks, they just didn't fit... and you know what, the first person I thought of was you.'

"THEN he tries to hand 'em over to me, but I didn't want any of it. And what do ya know, my manager walks in right then, with dirty ol' Rick tryin' to peddle me socks and underwear. Hahahaha! I was fired right on the spot, bud, GAAAAAAK!"

HAVING concluded this little tale, Remy vomited a bit and spat on the floor, aiming for a plant which I'm sure often served as his makeshift spittoon. Remy spoke like an overexcited rodent. His breathing was somehow a secondary function of his being. Between his gambling, drugs, alcohol and delirious, cockeyed fancies, there was a passionately destructive voice that sought to undermine all traditional values. He was a textbook Sanguinaire, alright.

THE kid had a new job every time I saw him and a new story to boot. He presented a strange moral compass that revered sleaziness and degeneracy above all else. And boy, was he fun to listen to. I guess tornado chasers always have something interesting to report back to the prairies.

HE had a corrosive hold over Cooter, and the rest of us couldn't help but partake in their hilarity. We all had a few more drinks, and then I summoned up the nerve to ask Remy what his deal was. I asked him as straight as I could, "So, if you don't mind me asking, why are you so fucked up?"

"WHATCHA mean, bud?"

COOTER intervened, "That's a pointed question, old sport… ease up."

"NO, no, no… don't get me wrong. I'm just trying to get a perspective on this whole thing. I haven't known you upstanding gentlemen all that long, and I figure I might as well take the chance to get to know our 'breed' better, especially in such extremes as yourself, Remy. What did you see in your vision again? I know you told me but I can't quite remember…?"

REMY answered me promptly, "What do you want me to tell ya, bud? I'm gonna get smacked by a car in the next few years and have my guts spill out all over the street! Or maybe you wanna hear that I like to follow creepy pedophile-looking schizos into the little boy's room for kicks and kicks alone? I do it 'cuz who gives a shit about anything we do. Nothing matters once ya know! So I have fun spitting back at this fucked-up world, and I'll do it for as long as I can, yo, before that car hits. It's my life and I'll ruin it however I want!"

I was surprised to hear such an uncharacteristically sensible answer find its way out of his mouth, and then I asked, "Do you think you'll beat it?"

REMY looked confused but still answered, "Nah, maybe, who knows… I don't wanna die, maybe that means I won't." He chuckled.

THE group began consorting amongst themselves. Cooter returned to the now-watery cocktail he'd forgotten and left to address the lineup of servers that were screaming at him. I sauntered over to Darius, hoping to talk to him more about what his dad wanted and what we could expect from this meeting.

HE looked ambivalent and just leered at the others, pretending to listen, but in reality I suspected he was just waiting to chat with me. I tried to strike a lightish tone. "I thought I'd bump into you here. How's that club soda?"

"IT tastes fine," he replied, without an inkling of good cheer. "I don't drink."

I was surprised, because I knew he was a junky. "But I just saw you crushing up Nepenthe with Remy over at Cooter's?"

HE replied curtly, "I never said I had an issue with drugs."

I wanted to challenge this contradiction, but he looked eerily serious.

"YOU look depressed, maybe a little sickly… you alright?"

DARIUS replied, "I dunno if being depressed is even a thing anymore. It just seems to be the default. I haven't been eating or sleeping, maybe it shows, but what's the point? I know it won't be the cause of my end. At least I have that certainty. Same thing with the drugs, I guess…"

I clarified, "Well, you know what I mean…we all feel like shit. You just look that little bit."

HE hesitated for a second then blurted out, "How'd you feel if you'd seen something you couldn't make heads or tails of, something you were forced to think about every day because it involved the most important decision anyone could ever make?"

I tried to reassure him. "I think we all feel that way, pal."

"NO! I'm talking about the *immediate*… Hell, you don't care."

I tried to look like I resented his comment and lent him an ear. "Go on with it, I'm interested... Between you and me, I'm not really the prick I pretend to be, it just makes it easier to avoid the people I hate or might end up hating. But fellow depressives like yourself, hell, you'll always have a place in the spot my heart ought to be…"

DARIUS summoned his courage and began again, "I haven't told anyone about this…" Then, staring right at me, he bared his soul. "I saw myself committing suicide."

"SHIT..." was my eloquent reply.

HE continued, "The fucked thing of it is, I've never once wanted to. I had a life that I'd built, I had friends, even a girl before the Event. But once I saw what I was inevitably gonna do, my depression just kinda kicked in. It just keeps weighing me down, heavier and heavier. I can't fight it anymore...

"I don't want to kill myself. I wish it could've been anything else! But I know that's what I'm gonna do… despite everything… The only reason I feel depressed is that I've seen myself already do it. It's a vicious snake eating its own rotten tail."

"FUCK, that's shit," was all I could say.

"YOU see what I'm saying? You see the spot I'm in?" He said this as a plea for an answer that I was too heartless to give right away, despite my recent attempts at being human.

I was tongue-tied for what felt like hours, but eventually came up with some false attempt at comfort. "It's a hell of a quagmire, that's for sure… Just hold out as long as you can. We're lucky to have enough autonomy and freedom to even think about this kinda stuff… You gotta ask yourself, why would we be able to do that if there were no answers for us to arrive at? We can figure this kind of shit out. Why else won't Cooter ever shut up about this shit? And your father, seems to me he thinks we might be able to change the futures we've seen, with science or something. Doesn't he think so?"

DARIUS'S eyes began to twinkle.

"REGARDLESS of what the Department thinks, we're in the best situation to handle shit like this. Who knows? It might even work out. We might be the ones capable of securing our own salvation. We can't determine how this is going to go." I hoped he would believe my bullshit, because I knew I certainly didn't.

COOTER clocked out and finished up by slamming a dirty dishrag down. He looked over at me and Darius and saw that we were getting emotional. He swooped in right as we were about to delve further into the abyss. He brought us back up to the terrible surface. He was in a fearsome mood. The man liked shouting war, and in a weird way I envied him for it.

"ALRIGHTY, mates, we gotta get to that meeting and see what these fuckers are gonna force us to overcome today!" Cooter declared.

WITH that, Darius reverted back to his morose, unassured self again, and I gave him a half shrug, not really knowing what he was going through, but detecting in myself the possible sensation of being moved.

Eight

"The end is built into the beginning." — Charlie Kaufman

Chipped teeth
Being single at a wedding
Being kidnapped and subsequently beheaded

WE shuffled along like lost souls, robbed of any chance to move gracefully beyond this earthly plane. Denied the ability to deny anything that mattered. We would have gladly welcomed a firing squad volleying accidental shots if it meant the chance to meet our end before the scheduled date of execution. We lined up at the same depressing church door, littered with cigarette butts, half-eaten chicken wings and plenty of other miscellaneous garbage.

THE crusty stains of fast food wrapping papers below me acted as a sort of unintended glue keeping the chipped wooden base of the door and its cracks sealed, forming a distinct greasy line between the holy and the corporeal streets. Finally, just as two pigeons began to wrestle over a putrid chicken nugget, the door opened. I spat on one of the pigeons as I walked in and watched the other one try to swallow the mucus that had landed on its fellow's eye.

WE hobbled in single file, picking up little fliers and leaflets as we walked down the garishly lit hallways that beamed with an ungodly glow of concentrated fluorescent light. As we approached the boiler room, I noticed a lunch box with a little Darwin fish sticker on it, perched atop this poorly assembled pile of photocopied handouts, the cover of which featured a family blissfully assembled in a free-loving circle with a benevolent Rectification leader at its centre. The title on each leaflet was "So you know when you're going to die?"

THE stack of papers was haphazardly thrown together on top of a dilapidated desk with rusted limbs. The desk wobbled in that annoying kind of way that makes it almost impossible to put anything on its surface and turn away with confidence. This was the pulpit of our Rectifier, to be sure. It was the cleanest thing in the room and the furthest from the boiler itself, so that there was no mistaking his holiness for the heathen rabble that ought not to attain celestial status.

OUR saviour soon arrived. Good old Ronald! He positioned himself behind his pulpit and greeted each of us with the hi's and hello's of a squawking seagull. I recognized in him the consolatory charm of a mortician.

WE seated ourselves upon the assembled chairs. Ronald glanced up at Cooter and made a marvelous noise resembling a cough that had lost its phlegm on the way up. Cooter's face was stained with a virulent sneer and dehydrated tears.

RONALD took out his tablet and began sifting through his meeting plan. I could feel that there was something special pulsating through his wiry and often unnoticeable lips that night.

"HELLO again, group. I'm happy to see old faces and new ones as well. If you are new here, welcome, my name is Ronald and I'm a Rectified Sanguinaire. Thank you all for joining me today and for your continued patience as we negotiate with the choir group to get our old room back."

"I'D like to start tonight's meeting by giving you all an insider's heads up." Here our savvy prophet assumed a hushed and confidential air. "As you know, these meetings are mandatory, but I feel I should warn you that the Department will be much more vigilant in reprimanding those of you who are unaccounted for in the upcoming weeks." Praise be unto thee, brave and blessed protector.

"FURTHER to the online notification, tonight's meeting is of particular importance. I will be distributing packages towards the end which contain the details of exactly what we will be discussing here, and all the changes and plans we have in store for the future, but first I'd like to do a group exercise." And in response to the groaning profanity with which these words were met, "Please try to keep aggressive and negative responses in check. Thank you all."

"NOW, I want each of you to express what it is about your vision that bothers you most and what you feel is the biggest barrier to your actively participating in society. I must remind you, we are here to learn and become better by listening to one another's responses to our shared affliction, so please concentrate your answers in a rational and productive way, okay, guys? Let's try to greet death with some positivity! Now, who would like to begin?"

RONALD waited, smiling eagerly through the silence. "Come now. Be brave. Who would like to start?"

UNAFRAID, the boiler poured forth its hurtling thuds and steam-searing rumbles, blessing us with a *phhhrrrring* of rust and bolts. It truly was the *Magic Flute* of furnaces.

AFTER several uncomfortable minutes, a disheveled-looking girl weighing about ninety pounds with black streams of mascara etched upon her cheeks timidly raised her hand. She began in a trembling voice, "Well, the worst part for me is the whole 'dying in childbirth' thing." She said this without an ounce of humor. "Like I told you guys before, I'm an escort, so getting knocked up is kind of an occupational hazard. But the thing is, I always thought I'd kinda like bein' a mom. Ever since my vision, I've been like a thousand times more careful with the Johns. I make 'em wear condoms every time now. I used to let it slide sometimes for the good paying customers, you know. Anyways, it's put a real damper on everything, and at this point I'm almost thinking, fuck it, why bother? I looked for other work for a while, but all the server jobs are already taken, and there's nothing else I'm good at. Besides, I like what I do. I keep people company and I make 'em happy. It's all I know and I like it. I don't got another way of 'actively participating in society.'" This was said with a roll of her eyes in Ronald's direction, but Ronald had stopped paying attention.

SHE sniffled and a black tear dripped down her face. "I know no matter what I do, someday soon I'm gonna trip and get knocked up. I'll never know if the next caller's gonna make the life that kills me. Every trick I turn could be a nine-month death sentence..."

HER sadness turned to malice. "Fuck it, maybe I'll quit. So I'll starve and be out on the streets. So what. I'll lock my goods up and let you dogs find some other leg to hump," the petite girl said this while looking down on all the men in the group as well as one lady admirer who was licking her lips.

AS usual, Ronald had missed his cue. I remember imagining that he was preoccupied by more important problems, like maybe he'd forgotten to put lettuce on the sandwich I could see sticking out of his lunch box and was wondering what kind of BLT it would be without the lettuce? A bacon tomato? What would that be? A BT?... Whatever mental quagmire he had been stuck in, Ronald eventually managed to jolt himself free of it and resume his rightful role. With a professional tone of feigned concern, he cooed, "It's Fatima, right…?"

"YES!" Perhaps she was agitated that he was focusing on how to address her rather than what she had said.

RONALD was not discouraged. "Fatima, you need to avoid concentrating on all the negatives of this experience. You have the power to overcome this anger. I see that it's crippling you and preventing you from being the mother that *I know you can be.* We all believe in you, don't we group? I know I sure do! So why not focus on the miraculous guarantee that you will bring a life into this world? Why let anything put a damper on that? Remember last week's assignment: let's try to think about the pleasant aspects of unchangeable situations."

FATIMA was furious. "What the fuck!" Tears welled up again in the girl's eyes as she continued, "What do you people even do?! Can't you understand that I would've loved to be a mom, but I can't feel anythin' but hate for my own unborn fucking child! Don't you think I feel bad enough about that already?!"

FATIMA sobbed, "I just can't do this anymore…"

"MAYBE you won't have it, fuck it, there are other options…" said the kind, if somewhat opportunistic, lesbian, winking wistfully.

RONALD used this emotional outpouring to burden the class with yet another of his infamous readied responses, "Let's all thank Fatima for sharing. We are all hurting, but hopefully we can help to shoulder each other's painful burdens and in this way, begin to heal. Now repeat after me: **What cannot be changed will not be changed. Things will be as they will**

be. I am powerless to control my end. Accepting this will put me on the path to empowered understanding."

DESPITE Ronald's efforts to get the whole choir singing, Cooter refused to utter a single syllable of the Department's slogan and just sat there, open-mouthed and aghast, as Cassandra's curse took hold of everyone else in the room. He steadied himself, looked the Rectifier square in the eye, and began his siege for the evening: "So is it my turn to talk 'bout my experience, Ronald?"

RONALD jumped in his seat, eel-like, then replied, "Cooter… I'm glad to see you're back and I'd love to have you contribute to our discussion. But please remember to abide by our safe-space policy and to respect the feelings of everyone else in the room. We don't want you getting carried away again."

"OH, don't you worry, Ronald, I'd never want to offend any of these folks. I got no qualms with the rest of 'em. My target's you."

RONALD tried to respond politely, "Once again… I don't think you understand what we're trying to achieve in these meetings. We don't want to promote hateful ideas, language or outbursts. That kind of behaviour is destructive, and it is my task to avoid it where I can. Instead, I want to help you to regain your autonomy. I want to get you to a place where you are able to determine the course of your life, instead of letting the Event and your affliction choose it for you."

THIS speech was uncharacteristically promising. Ronald had our attention for a moment and he knew it. We were listening. Cooter was listening. We were his for the converting, if Ron could only show us the way… Alas, the pressure proved too great. Ronald visibly crumbled under it and regressed to his disappointing norm, pollinating the room with a fungal spray of phony self-motivation: "Honestly, guys, the only thing stopping you is yourselves. The Event wasn't your fault, so don't let yourselves take the blame. Just look at me! It can get so. Much. Better. With a little time and a good old-fashioned try. Stick to it and you will be Rectified!"

COOTER predictably snapped, "The Event was my fault! It was your fault. It was the fault of every blind and blundering human being that came before us. It was the universe's reminder that maybe we've been neglecting *reality* too long. The Event was a last-ditch attempt to wake us up and force us to pay attention to what matters. It's not something we can decide to forget or tell to go away. And we shouldn't want to!"

UP until that moment, I hadn't realized that deep down this was how I felt about it all too. I sat back, stunned at this sudden surge of "caring" that was flooding through me. The group welcomed the interruption and a few people started to call out similar feelings. Ronald looked like a shifty rat caught midday who knows he's about to be crushed by an inescapable human foot. The ugliness of inevitability was about to come stomping down on him.

"AHEM, I don't think… I, um… well, that's not really very helpful… well, a good way to look at it, I find… I think… ummmm…"

I chimed in with what I thought was support for Cooter, "Sometimes it's about knowing that it won't be okay. Even if things can only get worse, shouldn't we confront them the way they actually are? Can't we at least acknowledge them? Maybe the Event was supposed to make us face the shitstorm that is the human condition. Face it head on. Maybe then the bullshit will stop and we'll find a way to function within the burden of these lives we never asked for."

RONALD tried to regain control. "This is exactly the kind of construed reasoning that exacerbates your affliction. I am afraid we may have triggered some radical thoughts and behaviour. I'm going to drop this exercise. I think the group would benefit more if we proceed to the second half of our meeting."

COOTER heaved a lamenting exhalation, first towards me, then in the direction of our leader.

HIS voice cracked as he tore into Ronald, "No! I don't believe a word of your goddamned pig shit and I don't think you do either. I say fuck getting together for Rectification. There's a real issue, and it matters, and we are going about fixing it the wrong way. Laertes, man, you're wrong too. It's not hopeless. The Event has given us the chance to find a loophole in our contract with fate. To prove once and for all that free will exists! That our choices matter! We should all be meeting to figure out how we're going to do it! How we're gonna free ourselves!"

I was offended by Cooter's optimism. It felt like the man wouldn't be appeased until he had hammered everyone in his proximity with his special brand of rose-coloured anarchy.

RAGE swelled up inside of me and I screamed back at him, "Then why hasn't anyone done it?! There's no record of a single person escaping what they saw so far! What makes you so goddam special? What was your vision? Just take a moment and tell me what that grim alleyway of fate looks like? Where's the fucking loophole? Tell me!"

MOST of Cooter's body froze, but his mouth immediately answered, "I don't need to take a moment. I know exactly what's gonna happen. I know exactly how I'm going to beat this thing."

BEFORE I could ask for clarification, he rushed on, "There's no such thing as inevitability. Every decision you make ripples a new series of changes. I had a vision. Everything I've done since has been a reaction to that vision. But it's been a deliberate fucking reaction. I've acted real goddam carefully. I'm starting a whole new chain of events. You're a fucking academic, Laertes. I shouldn't be lecturing you on causality."

HIS words were heavily loaded. There was an added layer of meaning to them all that I could feel but not quite understand, so I stayed quiet. Ronald seized the opportunity to stop us from pushing our cosmic battle any further. "Ahem, well, that was a productive little exchange, ladies and gentleman. Before the next meeting, let's all practice how to express our feelings with a little less hostility, shall we? Now, let's all thank Fatima, Cooter and Laertes for sharing, and we can move on with this evening's schedule."

COOTER stood up again. "Goddammit, man, this is life and death, this is not a fucking bad joke you can just choose not to laugh at!"

RONALD answered his misguided disciple meekly, "That's why we're doing Rectification therapy, Cooter. We know it's not a joke. We're trying to help. Please sit down…"

COOTER bit back, "No! I'm done with this fucking psychiatric approach. I don't care what you cock stains do to me anymore, quarantine me, detain me, whatever… you'll have to find me first. I'm done. There's just one more thing I gotta do – "

WITH that, Cooter leapt up and lunged at Ronald, decking him straight across the jaw. Ronald's lip burst open, splattering a constellation of bloody stars all over Fatima, who just happened to be sitting closest to him. Her adroit reaction to the spray indicated that she may have had some experience in dodging spontaneous showers.

RONALD fell to the floor, cowered into a ball and began sobbing quite loudly. I suspect he was banking on this as a sure way to garner group sympathy. He was mistaken, however; most of the group just laughed and one member snatched his sandwich.

COOTER gestured for Darius and I to follow him. Half his face looked brazen and determined, but the other half revealed that even Cooter might be scared of the embarrassment that was sure to follow him if we didn't. Or maybe he was thinking about the serious legal troubles he would now surely face, troubles which had been nonexistent just five minutes before…

IT was my first real chance to be part of a genuine band of buccaneers. I knew the Department would come down on me hard for colluding with an idiot like Cooter, but I couldn't resist. We strode out of the boiler room and through the church's grimy door. We felt like outlaws. We knew what we were doing was kinda cool, and just then that mattered more than anything. Cooter suggested we go get drunk in a park, and we readily agreed, but from that moment on we were all keeping a close lookout…

Nine
The Quest for the Golden Bike

Unappeasable anger
Failing to surpass the achievements of your parents
Claims that universal qualities are national traits

I watched a squirrel chewing something in small incremental nibbles. The cute rodent's tail twitched in contentment as it took in the feast. Then a bird came and grabbed the thing by the neck, gnashing and pecking through the breast of my puffy friend, and eventually chewing off the tail. I watched as the tail tumbled down to the ground and knew it would be yet another magical day.

I had been on a bender since the violent assault on Ronald's person and had failed to show up for any subsequent meetings. This had resulted in innumerable missed calls from the Rectification centre. I was trying to lay low. Drunk and low. I figured I might be off the hook legally for what had happened, but as far as the Department was concerned, I was aiding and abetting a known Sanguinaire, and I knew I'd be subject to their disciplinary measures at the very least. I visited my apartment sparingly, sleeping instead on whoever's couch I had spent the night with. These couches were my life rafts, keeping me adrift.

AFTER a few days, this pattern became dull, and so I started toying with the idea of going on an epic journey to no place in particular. The only destination I could dream up was anywhere but the here and now. Normally I lived in this sort of self-imposed poverty; call it Stoic, Brahmanic or Dervish… I had made enough money before the Event to maintain a modest and isolated lifestyle. My travels were usually confined to a small walking radius, only ever reaching as far as the local bus route's last stop, but now I wanted an adventure… It was a strange time. I knew something big was about to happen, and I knew that I was going to be at the centre of it…

EVENTUALLY my musings manifested themselves into a full-fledged commitment to be rid of the city. I was going to skip town. The rumour going around was that the Department's new enforcement branch was in full swing, and I thought I'd spotted some of them skulking around my block – that or my paranoia was back again. Either way, an immediate departure seemed the reasonable course of action, and I figured it'd be easy to abandon a life I didn't really have.

UNFORTUNATELY, though, I was in a bit of a bind. I wouldn't be able to hop on a flight or a train without having to register my psychological status, nor could I really afford such first-class extravagances. I needed to find a way out that wouldn't cost me too much money, so I decided on the poor man's mechanical chariot, and what do you know? I ended up finding a twenty-five-dollar bicycle online.

I dropped by my apartment and looked at my cat, who hadn't eaten for a day or two, and I split my last can of tuna with him. Then I headed out again and trotted down to Kensington Market. I rendezvoused with a bearded woman stashing boosted tires and broken bikes in her trunk. She was to be the salesman of my mechanized horse, and what an engaging gargoyle she was.

"HI there, we spoke earlier about the bike?"

"YEAH, which of 'em ya want?"

I hesitated, "The least bad of the worst, if at all possible?"

"I got just these here racers fer ya..." said the hair sticking out of her chin.

"SPLENDID!" I replied.

SHE presented me with a bouquet of busted bikes whose origin and age befuddled time and space. I selected my stallion and heaved it over my shoulders, with some assistance from its vendor, then thanked her sincerely for all of her help.

SADLY, a few blocks of riding revealed that my seemingly mighty steed was in fact somewhat lame, and certainly unrideable in its present condition. Thus I ended up spending most of my remaining silvers on its repair, which essentially equaled the initial purchasing price, but man, it was worth it. I looked down at my prize, and it shone with a fierce '90s charm that demanded awe and affection. You could tell it had once been considered someone's diamond, and it still had enough rattle left in it for a good long trip. Yessiree, the speed racer was ready for her not-so-maiden voyage, and so was I...

THE heat was intense that day and I didn't really have more than my one outfit, but my trousers were fit for fall and wouldn't be at all appropriate for a long ride. Luckily, I managed to find some used swimming trunks at the bottom of my bag, and I combined these with my only pair of shoes, which were pointy and elfish in style. I got them either for a wedding or a funeral – I can't remember...

I had mentioned something to Remy the day before about my desire to leave the city, and he had seemed to share my enthusiasm. I figured he'd be a welcome distraction on the journey, so I tracked him down and he agreed to join me. Darius had predictably declined my offer with a mopey shake of his head, but as long as Darius nested in the same home as old Bakhshi, I figured he'd be okay. As for Cooter, he loved the city too much to leave it, despite everything. He'd told me proudly that he'd been born in Toronto, a rarity all but lost these days, and that he had never left it once in his life. I was slightly surprised that his fear of leaving the city exceeded that of our current standing with the D.P.W., but I knew there was no reasoning with him.

REMY proposed we ride to Niagara Falls. He said he'd picked this destination because it shared a border with the US and might offer us a chance to jump over, but I think it's likelier that he got the idea from the cheap thrift store keychain I knew he owned with a little picture of the waterfalls. I was just driven by the adrenaline of it all, not knowing how long it would take, what route we'd follow, how or even if we'd ever get back. But I too was tantalized by the idea of jumping the border. We'd heard that the Bible Belt had gained enough of an angry hick force to repel some of the Department's influence and regulations, but I wasn't counting on it.

AND so it was that Remy and I set off for Niagara Falls astride shining and road-ready bicycles. We peddled for the first few hours with few complaints, but then our bodies experienced sharp shooting pains, beginning in the areas you'd expect and spreading, until eventually every part of our beings were unsafe to put pressure on. After five hours I felt a core discomfort in my loins and began to question my fertility prospects. But at least that one made sense. I was angrier at the stranger parts of me which were hurting. How the fuck does a toe ache to that startling a degree?!

IN spite of the pain, the clicking of gears and singing sting of warped tires on dry asphalt was giving me a real hard-on. The rumbling of it all titillated the inner recesses of my deranged and thirsty soul. It felt like the contraption might give way at any minute and leave me at the mercy of the highway traffic ripping past us. I'd have been terrified had I not already known how I was going to die. Surprisingly, Remy seemed just as unconcerned, if not more so. Despite the killer nature of cars in this kid's vision, I saw nothing but glee expressed every time I turned to look back at his dopey face. I gave him fifty percent odds of even making the journey, and I have to admit I felt a sick kind of curiosity to witness the fateful collision firsthand.

WE peddled hard down Satan's Service Road, which is what I had dubbed the infinite service line adjacent to the highway. You could see the searing tar of the road frothing in the sun's steaming heat for kilometres and kilometres... it was beautiful in its way.

MY ass calloused around the skewer-like seat and caused me endless frustration. Remy, however, had anticipated this and had brought a gel covering for his. I was skeptical as to where the cover had come from but decided not to ask. Eventually I had to stop and take a break from the pain. Remy came up from behind and silently handed me his sweat-soaked ass seat, bathed in the juices that had emanated from his crotch splint. It dripped profusely in his hand, and a single tear rolled down my face. Real compassion is sharing a sweaty ass seat.

AS we were readying to take off again, Remy looked at me and asked, "Yo, bud, I was wonderin' if you'd help me write this apology/guilt letter I gotta toss the courts. My probation officer's wantin' me to rethink my life, makin' up fer what I did, bud. I was figurin' you're the kinda guy who'd know how to use big words."

I laughed. "So you want a complete stranger to forge an admission of guilt for you to present to the courts?

"YESSIR!"

I prepared myself for the story I was about to unleash and asked, "Well, first I'd need to know how you got into this predicament. Would you honour me with the tale?"

REMY horked a larger than average slimy splurge of coagulated phlegm and began excitedly, "So I was in the middle of one of my crazy benders, it was around 5AM and I was racking lines when I hear this creak coming from my back door."

"SO here I am, bud, just treatin' myself to a buffet of illicit goodies, when I see but this little puff of tangled hair pop up from behind me. And it turns out I know the fucking guy breakin' in! He's a dishwasher at one of the kitchens I deal drugs to. I reckon an ol' fling of mine must've told 'em the doors were always unlocked 'cause she worked at the same place for a while.

"I guess you can never know for sure, but please, carry on," I pleaded.

WITH ferocity in his beady eyes, he shouted, "Oh yes, I do know for sure! I could feel 'er in the thing! So anywayz... I see this goof and he has this white-trash thug of a friend, and they're both just lookin' at me. I call these kinda folks 'Yo Buds', bud. They're like white trash, fetal alcohol syndrome, wannabe gangsters. They're always pale, pasty and sweaty, usually got terrible acne, and these ugly little bodies hidden in their baggy hoodies. You know?"

I nodded, but apparently it was unconvincing, and my companion felt the need to go on: "Ya, bud, you must've seen 'em! They always got somethin' to prove and they fight as a way of talkin'. Plus they gotta out-tough the gangsters they're tryin' to be so they act even worse than the real criminals of the hood. They always got these little squealing voices too, an' hit their highest pitch when they're threatenin' to knock you out! They're always claimin' they got a brother in jail who'll get ya when he's free. Fuck, there's a whole bunch of these street skids, bud. Trust me, I know... I used to run with 'em!"

I nodded more vigourously this time. "okay, back to my story... I'm like, 'What the fuck are you doing in my house?' And the guy I know is like, 'Yo, Bud, I ahhh, thought you were maybe up to chill... I just wanted to pick up an eight ball...' For a second I thought maybe they really had just slipped in to pick up the goodz, but then I was like nah... they would've had money in hand and double-rattled the wire I hooked up to my window for late-night calls.

"SO then I kinda pushed the one guy back into the kitchen a bit, and then I see the fuck I don't know readying to boost my stash, bud!

"SO'S I took one of my butcher knives and swiped at the two of 'em, then the dishwasher backs up and begs me to stop by offerin' me some pills in exchange for me not guttin' 'em. If they'd just wanted to party from the start, we coulda had a hoot – there's always enough to go around... but kids these days, I tell ya... no brains and no respect."

I found it hilarious that he referred to them as kids, considering his own age, and had to stop myself from telling him that he in no way seemed to differ from these "yo buds" in personality, speech, attire or action... Plus the story was funny in its own right, and after rolling hysterically for a bit, I tried to calm down and listen again.

HE went on, "Now I'm standin' there with a bag of pills in front me an' holding these criminals up with my knife. What's a fella to do when he's almost been robbed an' there's a whole bag o' drugs dangling out in the open like that, just take one or two? Nah, bud, nah… I snatched the whole bag! I robbed the fucks that were robbin' me! And then I called the cops and held the goofs there at knife point! Hahahahahahaha! I figured, what are they gonna do? Tell the cops I stole their drugs? Hahaha!"

I implored him to finish, "But the cops did in fact arrest you in the end? I'm guessing that's where this story is heading?"

HE artfully ejaculated another hork and went on, "Yeah… I tried to hide the worst of it, but they somehow saw the drugs, blood and a hooey of other shit in my shack. I tried to tell the cops it belonged to those fucks, but they wouldn't have it and just arrested the bunch of us to be safe and to be pricks."

"I asked 'em if I could change and put on my only suit before we got in their cop car… I guess they weren't really bad guys, cuz they ended up lettin' me. It was a swanky navy blue pinstripe with a helluva lapel, an' I wore it with a billiard ball decked-out tie that went along real nice, bud. I figured I'd be seein' a judge at some point, so why not look sharp? When they went to read me my rights, I told 'em there was no need. I already knew how the song went, bud. But most of the time it dun' really matter what you know 'cause they still up end throwin' you in the bull pit either way."

I had to ask: "What the fuck's the bull pit?"

REMY smiled devilishly with what looked like a pre-hork festering where his tooth should've been and explained, "That's where they collect all the scum from the slums and sewers of the street. They bring 'em to this dark underground pit before seeing a judge, bud. There you got murderers and molesters right beside drunk drivers and nice clean businessmen who isn't never got in any trouble before and only forged a few cheques or somethin' stupid like that.

"GAAAK! There are literally rusty metal bars 'round this huge cage, an' they got this little slot that the officers throw cheese on bread through. Sometimes they even toss in tuna sandwiches. Those are worth fighting for, let me tell ya, and that's usually where the trouble starts, bud. You get these gangster demons with shanks shoved up their asses just so they can get the good sandwiches. Oh sure, they'll cut ya for a chance at getting the tuna ones. He who controls the tuna runs the pit!"

I had almost forgotten that we were even riding by this point, and I asked the kid, "How many times have you been invited to the bull pit?"

REMY replied, "Many many times, I gotta say... but every time I learn a thing or two! Anywayz, I finally saw a judge an' I could tell he knew my arrest was fuckin' uncalled for, bud, and I could see the cocksucker was glad his little lackeys had dragged me through the ringer all the damn same. Eventually he sentenced me to probation on the condition that I admit some guilt for robbin' the robbers of their 'property'. So anyways, now I gotta write the apology letter I was telling you about. You in or what?"

I decided I owed him a good deed in return for the entertainment his debacle had afforded me. "Sure, why not. I'll do it if we ever get back there. I have nothing better to do with my life. Then again, I might be just as juicy a candidate for detainment as you are at this point. We are both psychiatric fugitives in the eyes of the Department. If it'll help at all, I'll do it, but I gotta tell you, I think we're fucked either way."

REMY replied, "Thanks, bud. I figur' it's just another thing that'll give the Department that much more reason to hate on me. I'd appreciate it if you'd write it. Besides, I reckon the heat'll pass on us soon, bud. The Department isn't gonna waste that much money and resources chasing down a coupla hoodlums like us. With them, it's about what it costs to go after ya, and what they'll get if they catch ya. If it costs more than you're worth, they'll just look the other way. There's no benefit in it for them, see? That's capitalism for ya! Man, you gotta love it… At the end of the day, they're just a business, yo."

AFTER having digested all this in the sweltering heat, I decided to lead the charge and peddle harder for a while. We continued our ride along that eternity of tarmac and were greeted by dark, stormy clouds that cast a dim mutant rainbow. We weren't scared of a storm – hell, we were ready to ride through a hurricane – and Remy seemed mirthfully prepared to meet his maker.

I won't keep you in suspense any longer. Our twelve-hour trek was not to be his end. We made it to the falls and checked into our motel. It reeked of stale kitchen products and burnt coffee. The floors were sprinkled with splotches of either blood or wine. I dealt with the inept concierge, Pete, who evidently took great pride in his little red name tag, and managed to get us a room with two beds in it. The second we lay down, we immediately fell into the righteous sleep of the weary traveller.

IN the morning I decided to forego the waterfall in hopes of crossing the border. We'd catch one of the world's greatest natural marvels some other day, likely as not…

Ten

"And death shall have no dominion." – Dylan Thomas

Being told your girlfriend is pregnant
People who call out their own name
Doctors that exchange pleasantries with you before telling you that you have cancer

REMY and I got back to Toronto a few days later, exhausted, withered and utterly defeated. We had attempted in vain to cross the border but had met with awful and uncompromising rejection. I'd figured the Department would eventually put restrictions on our passports. I just hadn't anticipated how quickly they'd be about it. I'd thought we'd kind of be low priority for them. But they cared about us alright, and I was starting to suspect there'd be no end to the consequences of Cooter's violent behaviour.

UPON our return, we found that felon wallowing, lout-like, in a corner. He spotted Remy and I at the fire escape and just stared vacantly at us for a while before finally letting us in. "What do ya want? Can't you see I'm busy?"

"YER just sitting there in yer boxers with a ketchup stain on yer shirt, bud… What the fuck were you even doin'?" Remy inquired.

TAKING a swig from a can of beer whose bottling fee likely exceeded the value of its beloved contents, Cooter returned, "Is that a wire you're using as a belt?"

WITH a roguish air, the street kid smirked and corrected him, “Close, it’s a plastic string, bud! I found it caught up in my bike tire… speaking of bikes, me and Laertes had a real trip… you missed out, bud. GAAAAK!.”

COOTER just sighed and crumpled into his dilapidated chair.

“WHAT’S the matter with ya, eh, bud? You look even lower than usual. You’ve been hanging around with that bindlestick Darius, I bet. He’s a real downer, bud.”

COOTER moaned, “Nope… haven’t seen him. Haven’t seen anyone. Spent the last few days devourin’ every substance I could get my hands on an’ dodgin’ mysterious knocks at the door. If I poke my head up and go outside, the Department might nab me, and if I stay in here thinking about all this shit, I’ll start to go insane…

“I don’t know, fellas, it’s fuckin’ embarrassing all things considered, but I’ve been thinking my only chance at avoiding the steaming pile of shit that purports to be my future is a sit-down with Professor Bakhshi…”

CLEARLY something had upset Cooter to his core; otherwise, he’d have never considered talking to Darius’s father. He kept glancing furtively at me, and I felt too uncomfortable to say much.

REMY was more communicative: “*GAAAAAAAAKKKK!!!!!!*”

COOTER’S spirits were lifted for a moment by this cheerful expulsion of viscous-like liquid. “Well, shit, Sir Remy. It’s good to have you back! So what do you say, boys? Think it’s time we talked to that pompous wind bag? Thing is, we’re gonna need Darius to make the introductions. He’s prolly at his old man’s house…”

COOTER turned to me with an expectant look that said, "It's your job, go get him. I did enough by coming up with the idea." I gave in. "Alright, I'll try to find him. But I don't see why I'm being honoured with the charge. I barely know the gangly depressive."

COOTER was quick to answer, "Ya, but I saw you two gloom baskets exchanging sorrows at the bar while I was workin'. He trusts you. God knows why… I'll text you the address."

SO off I went, choosing to disregard the paranoia and festering distrust oozing from my companion's farewell...

THE sky that afternoon was a depressing mess. It gave off a cancerous gloom that saturated the dingy sidewalk and sad, featureless structures. The buildings I passed must have been constructed in a deliberate attempt to capture architectural ugliness in its purest form. They were these 1970s beige-coloured, gargantuan monstrosities and provoked an inspiring degree of revulsion.

THIS was Dawes and Danforth. "The other side of the tracks," as I affectionately referred to it. It was about as far from Eden as you could get, travelling eastward, of course, but my dismal surroundings weren't really the problem…

I was trying to wrap my head around just how I'd been recruited for this ludicrous mission. I felt like a loser who'd actually called in to one of those late-night televangelist God-gabbing hotlines that lets you join their Jesus club so long as you can afford it, and with the crippled zeal of a hopeful grandmother, I had pledged myself for only $9.99! I'd have considered the whole thing a farce just a few weeks back, but now I could feel myself getting carried away by delusions of making a difference, and maybe even delaying my date with death. Cooter's wager had acquired Pascalian proportions, and

I was beginning to believe. He'd convinced me that it was time to act, and here I was, acting. But I still felt like an idiot.

AT one point I passed a slew of rundown shops and saw this sad little shop trying to pawn itself off as a children's bookstore. There, staring at me through the greasy glass, was a tarnished book leaning on a once-translucent windowpane. Its cover featured a sad teddy bear with the title *Something Lost.* Christ…

I finally reached the claustrophobic borough of Toronto that was East York. Pickled by the 1950s and bereft of any of the charm that the rest of the city had, its only real draw was the comparative affordability of its houses (the rest of the city had been hijacked by a coalition of greedy landlords, making it virtually uninhabitable). According to Cooter, this was where I'd find the most depressed member of our sad little gang. But you could hardly blame Darius for his despondence.

I couldn't stop thinking about his suicidal paradox and it wasn't even my suicide. Death to me was just this total and absolute surrender of self. Neither an end nor a beginning, just a silence collapsing in on itself... And to be forced into volunteering for it! It was just too miserable… "If the immediate and direct purpose of our life is not suffering, then our existence is the most ill-adapted to its purpose in the world." What a guy that Schopenhauer was.

I arrived at the house and knocked on the door. Darius opened it and invited me up to his room. Inside was a teenager's soggy mess, littered with trinkets from his youth that belonged in a box buried deep and forgotten somewhere in the basement.

HE had a collection of posters featuring anti-establishment rock bands, an Xbox and an old soccer team photo hung crookedly on his wall. The photo displayed a much healthier version of Darius, a version that had yet to be cradled into total resignation by the loving arms of anemia and excessive drug use.

PRESENT-DAY Darius seemed to pick up on my uneasiness and suggested we take a walk. I agreed. I would have agreed to anything. I felt an uncharacteristic need to buy the kid a puppy or an ice cream or something. And I would have done it too, if I'd thought it'd make a lick of difference. He looked like a fucking prisoner of war. I could see his ribs through the sweat-stained, potato-sack-like poncho he was wearing, and he had these blackened rings of raccoon-like banditry encircling his eyes. His beard was twisted and gnarled and dangling like Long John Silver's might. His legs were just two scrawny twigs of skinned-over bones. Yeesh.

I felt honesty would prove the most effective tactic and remarked accordingly, "It looks to me like you have the whole ensemble going: lack of hygiene, terrible attire, the works… all you need is a little soot on each cheek and you're all set."

HE replied morosely, "I just don't care anymore."

"GOT it… Well, here I am, your friendly neighbourhood Sanguinaire, just checking in. No one's heard from you in a while. Wasn't too sure you'd still be here, but I'm glad you are. We need your help, kid."

THE kid didn't answer and I didn't want to push him, so we strode along in silence until we hit the entrance of the Don Valley and turned our steps toward a little park slouched into its hillside. The park's playground was designed like a sea ship and titillated the inner sailor in me. I soon felt right at home, a stowaway tucked underneath the hull of this great vessel. I focused my attention on Darius again and spoke to him thusly: "Look, I get that you're in a shit position, but I've been thinking… maybe you should work this thing from Cooter's point of view? Why not try the whole free will bit and just say fuck it… Don't go through with it. Simple as that."

HE had a gloomy answer ready for me: "Don't bother, Laertes. I've gone through all the possibilities. Ok, listen: I think I've found a way to describe my impending suicide: it's like a career for me now. I never wanted this job but It's the one I ended up with. I live with It day in and day out, constantly at the forefront of all my thoughts.

"I keep trucking on through It, learning to deal with It as a fact of life. I've started to accept all the petty stresses and reliefs that It entails, just like I would with any job, and you know what's fucked? Part of me's even starting to like It. It's familiar now. I've got a solid routine of procrastination down. I put It off every time it comes up in any serious way, but I know one day I'll be numb enough to stop avoiding It, and I'll schedule that last appointment.

"YOU understand, right? There's nothing left of who I was before. It defines me. I wouldn't be able to live without It. I've forgotten how to do or be anything else… So there's no sitting myself down and telling myself not to. Each day I'm more and more eager to finish what I've started. That's just how it's gotta be. And to tell ya the truth, I'm tired... No one ever thinks about how exhausting a thing like this is. I'm telling you, it's a career, man."

I tried to summon up a convincing reprimand. "So that's it? You're going to give up? Just like that? You're going to lie down and die? Maybe what you saw was a warning, a chance to make things different, you know? Shit, man, people change careers all the time!" I could hear myself repeating Cooter's sound-bites.

DARIUS shrugged and replied, "Maybe that's true for you. I hope so. But my game's fixed, and I won't pretend it's not. You have to play the cards you're dealt, even if the deck's rigged. Please don't bother me about it anymore. It's not that serious in the grand scheme of things."

IRONICALLY, up until this point, I'd been successfully repressing any issues I might have had with my own sense of mortality. But something about the calm way this kid was talking about his end, metaphor heavy as the talk was (was death a job or a hand of bridge now?), provoked a real sense of fear in me, and the sting of it made me cry out, "Wrong! What could be more serious than ending your life, man?!"

HE replied quietly, "Honesty, self-awareness...."

WE sat in silence for a moment, and then the kid's face began to change a tad before my eyes. His jaw hardened. Determination was creeping into every pointed corner of that sallow and angular profile. Sure enough, brave words followed: "We can't change what's going to happen to me, but it isn't over for the rest of you. It's too big a coincidence, you coming by today. There's gotta be something behind the timing of it all..."

"WHAT are you talkin' about?"

"WELL, last night this Department guy came by the house. He came late, I'm talking four or five in the morning, but of course I haven't slept in days cause of the whole all-consuming suicide thing. So I'm up and I hear these muffled voices. I peek my head out and see this old geezer who used to work with Dad. They were real chummy back in the day. I never liked the clear-eyed son of a bitch, but I know he's high up there, might even be the director by now, so I listen in close..."

"HE starts talking about some new kind of Nepenthe they've manufactured, saying how it's specifically designed to counteract Sanguinaire immunity. He's all excited, claiming it's the final solution to our affliction.

"NOW you talked with him long enough to know my pops always had kind of an issue with their whole 'medicate first, ask questions later' way of thinking, but I guess he hasn't made much progress doing things his way, and I think my never-ending stream of disappointing behaviour coupled with his lack of success may have dimmed his principles a little. I know how much he misses the glory days, back when he was a scientific pioneer..."

THIS was easy for me to believe, and I wondered how often the greedy need for scientific truth outweighed the value of the life that's sacrificed for its display.

"ANYWAYS," my skeletal informant resumed, "I guess the Department got sick of waiting for the Sanguinaire condition to sort itself out, and the drugs they had couldn't be made any more effective, so they sent a team to find a new kind of medication, and find it they did. A plant that yields a whole new kind of Nepenthe. A flower, shit, I don't know flower names, what was it called... lettuce?"

"LOTUS?" I suggested.

"YEA, that was it! But there aren't many of these lotuses growing naturally, so they've only got a bit of this Nepenthe 2.0 so far. No, Nepenthe-X. That's what he called it. So they've been doing everything they can to synthesize the plant's properties. Until then they can't make more than a tiny little batch of this new and improved mental equalizer. They're desperate to get the thing mass produced, and they've recruited Dad to help."

"MENTAL equalizer, eh? Catch any other details on what's so different about this new stuff?"

"MMMM, there was a bunch of scientific jargon, man. It 'rewires neural pathways' something something. As far as I can make out, it's supposed to shoot pleasure into your brain whenever you thought about dying or the Event, not just make you indifferent like the other stuff did. Thinking about death and fate is going to turn into something peaceful, even pleasant. Only it turns out there are side effects in some cases. My dad tried to get details but the guy was being real evasive."

"THAT sounds menacing. Your father's just going along with it?"

"SOUNDS like it. He put up a bit of a fight at first. But his ol' medical colleague just said stuff like, 'Should we really risk letting these victims suffer just because we disagree on methods and forms of treatment? These people are sick, we don't have time to let things get any worse…' Etcetera, etcetera. Then he threatened Dad's position at the university and eventually he gave in."

DARIUS'S initial surge of determination proved to be contagious, and I'm embarrassed to say I felt the flames of revolution flaring up inside me. "So what are we going to do? I don't want to be medicated with shit like that."

DARIUS gave me the answer I think I already knew was coming. "You have to bust in and destroy the shit. All of it. They've been testing it a bunch, so there's not much left. My dad's got what's left in his lab at the university. It'll be safeguarded by Department officers, but I think I have a plan that'll get you in. It'd be a piece of cake if I thought we could get my pops on board, but I can't risk giving him another chance to be a decent human being, let alone a father."

I accepted my mission with a surprising lack of self-criticism. It immediately became something matter of fact. It was going to happen. I was going to do it. I was going to say fuck you to the Department and save my brethren by giving them a chance to live out their miserable lives, safeguarding the inalienable rights of my fellow citizens, guaranteeing that each of them would have to think about their deaths and feel just as wretched about them as we did. After this surge of civic vigour, I was struck by the inconsistency of Darius's conduct and prodded for clarification. "What do you get out of all of this if you're just going to off yourself? Don't you want to live to see how it all plays out? Maybe that's something worth watching? For destruction's sake?"

"NO… I'm going to kill myself."

IN a final appeal for the world of the living, I implored, "What about everybody else? What about your father? That prick loves you, Darius. It'll kill him."

DARIUS looked at me, unconcerned, and just replied, "Maybe, maybe not. But love's not enough in this world, Laertes, it's just not enough..."

Eleven

The Myth of Sisyphus

Whiskey as a remedy for a child's illness
Relatives who don't come back from war
Sticky thighs

I left Darius, not knowing if, or when, he would really go through with the suicide, or how I'd feel about this free will and fate mess if he did.

HELL, I'd already seen enough proof that our lives had been pre-written by an all-powerful apathetic scribe, but watching another Sanguinaire drop out of the battle at this stage in the game was bound to push me over the edge a bit. I didn't know if I could deal with this particular unsung casualty... but I was condemned to complete the quest he had sent me on.

I hid out for a few hours digesting it all and eating a pack of discarded, unopened cheese sticks that I'd been lucky enough to come across. I contemplated the futility of life and thanked Darius for the renewed predominance of my morbid meditations.

I kept lapsing into different frenzies of thought, considering the consequences of this new form of Nepenthe and what it meant for me and my ragtag collection of disenfranchised Sanguinaires. I couldn't stop thinking about the value I placed on my "awareness" of the end, and how it compared to my fatalistic friend's affection toward his suicide. Were these values misplaced? Was I gaining anything from my preoccupation with death? Yes, dammit! It was *my* preoccupation, I had a right to it... I'd gotten used to it! What right did anyone have to deprive me of my misery? Just like Darius...

IT was like owning some defective device, a vacuum cleaner or any other piece of equipment that's long exceeded its expiration and now exhibits a curious array of defects that only you know how to fix. A kick here, a tug there. There's this intimacy between you and that broken vacuum. Only you can make it work... It was my broken mind, and I didn't want to lose it.

MY cheese sticks ran out and I thought it was high time to start my expedition in earnest. I ventured back to Cooter's and decided to bypass the crackheads on the front stoop this time, guarding the door like Scylla and Charybdis, devouring every daring sailor that passed along in a whirlpool of begging, foul banter and meaningless attempts to strike up meaningless conversations. I lacked both the patience and time to devise explanations for not having a lighter or pocket change.

AND so I scaled the fire escape like everyone else and in that moment felt truly initiated into Cooter's intimate circle. Looking through the window, I was relieved to find my companions shambling around in a blissful stupor of self-defeat and staggering drunkenness, and I suspected they hadn't come up for air since I'd left them. I knocked on the window and they let me in.

AFTER going over most of my encounter with Darius, sans the suicide parts, I was glad to see flickers of glee in Cooter's face and to hear his ready commitment to help. Remy was largely indifferent, but I knew he could be bribed with intoxicants and made him some seedy promises.

DARIUS had suggested that we head to the lab and try to scout it out first. He had a pretty good idea of which hallways and rooms we needed to head for and had drawn us a squishy little map on a dingy napkin. We knew that we would need disguises and started hunting through Cooter's cupboards and drawers for appropriate hats, sunglasses, hooded sweatshirts, etcetera. He had a pretty good collection, stained and strange-smelling, of course, but with everything on we weren't easy to recognize. Remy kept pushing for wigs but was overruled.

DISGUISES ready, it was time to plan the finer points of our reconnaissance mission. We decided that it would be better to head there during regular daylight hours. We figured the nighttime guards would probably be easier to spook and more trigger happy, and anyone walking around at night would automatically seem suspicious. Cooter proposed we head over around 1 PM, and we agreed. Those guards would be relaxed, verging on complacent. They'd have just had lunch. Their eyelids would be droopy. And the possibility of three repulsive and debauched renegades enacting a haphazard mission of sabotage would appear remote indeed. As luck would have it, this lovely piece of reasoning also gave us a fifteen-hour window in which to drink ourselves into an oblivion from which no man could escape unscathed...

WHEN that fateful, golden, midday hour arrived, our horrid hangovers were mingled with a strange sense of confidence and good cheer, and we slithered through the city bowels, using alleyways and side streets like the shady yellowbellies we were. I directed them to the lab and we entered through its western entrance in accordance with our napkin map.

THE building we entered was Soviet-like in style, and the hallways had just the most dazzling pinch of grey sterility to them. The whole structure felt both clinical and office-like, and you could feel that it had been designed with efficiency and well-measured budgeting in mind. I remember thinking that most modern buildings seemed to have this same uniform aesthetic: the mood is empty and accented by the most unnoticeable objects... neat and tightly prepared with these strategically placed chairs, a minimalistic table and, maybe, if you're lucky, a "cubist by number" puked-out painting hanging on the wall, proudly displaying its computerized assemblage of shades placed within a mathematically engineered scheme. I hated it.

WE turned a corner and were stopped dead in our tracks by the majestic appearance of the Shah look-alike himself. He somehow saw through our bespectacled camouflage and arrested us with his eyes. We were helpless prisoners. And with a look, he motioned us into a crowded classroom filled with downcast and despondent would-be listeners. They didn't look like your typical student crowd, and I realized the professor must have called in his new Sanguinaire recruitments. I felt panic creep over me. It was a trap. It had to be. The old bastard had gotten us all together and was going to hand us right over to the Department for testing or confinement or some other fucked-up purpose. And we had walked right into it...

THE professor closed the door behind us, and I was summoning up the nerve to push past him and make a run for it when he locked eyes with me... I felt immediately that this was not the same man I had met weeks earlier. There was almost more pain on his stately face than I could bear to witness. His eyes, once proud and fiercely intelligent, now seemed to express only shame and rage. I knew then that Darius was dead. And I knew that he knew that I knew...

HE made his way to the front of the room, glanced at each of us, and began, "The only thing we have sometimes is anger." He said this with a quiet and terrifying conviction that sent shivers down my spine. Beginning again, "It's one of the most honest of our emotions because it's unpleasant, and yet we allow ourselves to be seized by it. The pain that it brings does not dissuade us. Nor does the lack of any possible positive outcome. Unlike our pleasures, we gravitate towards anger not because it makes us feel right, but because we realize we need something from it, regardless of the ramifications. We need its brute strength, its all-consuming focus of vision, and so we use it even though it hurts us, we cradle it even though it eats away at our decency, and we protect this feeling despite the fact that it might kill us.

"ANGER is our most primal reaction to injustice, and often it is the most powerful instrument we have to set things straight again. No one wants to admit this ugly truth. We have been trained to avoid that which is ugly. But the power of anger remains nonetheless."

I knew that in that moment all three of us shared the vehemence of the professor's call to arms and stood greedily awaiting more. We had forgotten all about the mission. He went on, "Now each of us will encounter many injustices in the course of our lives. Pain, death, sickness, corruption – these have existed for centuries, but our generation has had to bear an added burden. Our freedom has been violated by the grim truths that the Event revealed to us... Are any of you familiar with the tragedy of Sisyphus?"

I nodded. Cooter sniffed. Remy belched. "Sisyphus was a mythic hero, condemned by the gods and tasked with the eternal charge of repeatedly pushing a boulder up a mountain. Sisyphus would toil up that excruciating trail each and every day, over sharp shards of broken rocks and in torturous blistering heat, until he eventually reached the top. Only to repeat it all again a moment later."

"I put it to you that this is a metaphor for our existence: **a useless struggle toward nothing**. Our lot was assigned before we existed, and our fate is an endless return to non-existence.

We are cogs in a wheel that serves no end beyond the production of more cogs... Of course all of this has been said by countless people a thousand times over. The only difference now is that we've been shown the truth of it with a crueler clarity than ever before, and we're being forcibly programmed to forget it all."

THERE he was, dishing out the whole gunk of the universe. It was damn near poetic, I say... damn near. It was the most beautiful lecture I had ever been privy to. He was teaching us our own pain. And he just kept on teaching. "Camus had a slightly different way of looking at Sisyphus. On the outside, he said, the whole thing seems hopeless, but what people fail to acknowledge is the scorching impetus of his drive to get that boulder to the top. There he is struggling away, day after day, with nothing to look forward to but the endless task of getting that rock over the threshold, but each time, when he reaches the top of the mountain, Sisyphus smiles as he hurls the boulder over his head... do any of you know why?"

WE stayed silent. "Because every time Sisyphus gets that boulder to the top, he has a brief moment of respite before it falls, and that second gives him the chance to raise his middle finger to the gods and shout a sweeter slew of righteous insults than any of us can even imagine. He laughs at them, at their efforts to condemn him, and therein lies his vindication. Every day he taunts the gods and lets them know that he's immune to their cruelty. He takes pleasure in this eternal revenge. Nothing and no one can take that pleasure away from him. He will smile until the end of time, proving over and over that he can't be beaten by the wretchedness of fate. I have come to realize that this is the true strength of the Sanguinaire condition."

THERE was such infectious hope emanating from these hopeless words, and it permeated every being in the room.

He was uttering the exact sentiments we didn't even know we had. In that instant, the professor spoke to the inner gamut of our wailing pains and gave us a reason to fight back, a drive to push our own boulders, regardless of how useless it might be.

PROFESSOR Bakhshi had crossed the Rubicon and must have known what lay in wait for him as a result… "I'm here to help. It's time we made use of *our* affliction," he exclaimed with stalwart daring.

IT really meant something to hear the professor admit he shared *our* condition.

HE continued with what I realized was his swan song, "We're not fighting in order to face death… rather, we are coming back from death to face life. I won't abandon my right to see and reflect upon my own tragedy… Not too long ago, I witnessed the religious riots. I saw firsthand the turmoil they caused and the negative effects they had. Whether or not there was any merit to their arguments was immaterial, because the way these religious communities were handling the Event was violent and homicidal. The sign from God that they had been waiting for had turned into the reckoning of their entire system of belief.

"AT the time I couldn't help but side with my academic training over this supernatural embracing of hostile discord. I wanted to prevent any more fanaticism and curb the widespread acts of radicalized behaviour. I need you to understand what my options were. I need someone to understand why I've gone along with the Department this long. I could never make him see it… just like I could never hear what he was trying to tell me… But maybe you will accept my explanation…"

THERE was an uncomfortable and confused silence here, and I suspect that myself and Cooter were the only two in the room who knew who "he" was, unless Remy was also thinking of Darius under the guise of picking his nose with an absentminded appearance, but Bakhshi was lost in his own sadness and didn't seem to feel the awkwardness. After a few moments, he managed to catch his train of thought again and went on.

"THE current director of the Department is an old friend of mine, Dr. Kurzov, and he was almost exclusively responsible for the theory that the Event was a part of some collective mental illness. After they had quelled the riots, the Director and the Department filled a very painful void and told people what they needed to hear in order to carry on. I think Dr. Kurzov was trying to create global unity with his presentation of the Event as a collective sickness. Regardless, religion was out. Science was in. The people rejoiced, and I was among the celebrators.

"I was one of the few who believed that it was a good idea to have a community of experts discussing the Event, trying to understand where it came from, how it worked. Then the Sanguinaire condition emerged, and in response Dr. Kurzov pushed more and more medication, making it increasingly difficult for real conversations to take place.

"AS time went on, those afflicted grew worse – well, I don't have to tell all you that. The Nepenthe wasn't doing its job. But my attempts at therapy weren't working either, and so many of the afflicted were so repulsive… Worthless. Lazy. Many of them had been this way before the Event as well as afterwards, and it became so hard for me to pity him…"

THE professor looked at me, and I suspected he was about to approach the ultimate cause of this confession. "My son… he told me he was going to end his life. It was a part of his vision… and I did nothing. I just denied that it was going to happen. I was too busy looking for ways to treat him and everyone like him. I thought that was enough. He was constantly asking me for more. I hated him for it. And now he's gone…"

COOTER spat, "Bah." Then, turning to me, he said, "It all makes sense now, it's all coming together..."

MY face must have reflected my confusion and disapproval, but he didn't back down. "Don't you get it? His suicide, it all makes sense! Oh my fuck, I can't believe you don't see it!!!"

I tried to shush the brute. "See what!? What am I missing here?"

HE pressed on, "Darius was supposed to kill himself. It was the only way his father would help us, and now we'll actually be able to stop the Department's bullshit! His vision and his death were for us… Don't you get it? The wonderful and fucked up thing about Darius's suicide is that it wasn't for nothing. There's such an obvious reason for it, for all of it, the visions, everything… All we have to do now is act and we can prove it to the world! That's why he died, that's why we're here, that's what this is all about!"

I'D had enough of these paradox speeches. The way I see it is this: there's the way things are and the way things ought to be… No man has the right to confuse the two just because he prefers the way it makes him feel.

THE professor had brought me close to something, but Cooter's response sent me reeling away again in the opposite direction. I wanted to distance myself from all the Sanguinaire bullshit. I was feeling at odds with the whole damn condition. There comes a point where attempting to figure out the rhyme and reason of the universe loses its appeal, and I'd reached it.

THE fact that Cooter didn't even care about Darius's death because it fit nicely into his cosmic scheme showed exactly how dangerous this condition was. Who cares about making sense of death if it makes you care so little when it happens to someone you know? What the fuck does any of it matter then?

COOTER kept quiet once he realized he'd lost me as an audience member. We returned our attention to the prof and listened as the man delivered his son's eulogy. "I feel so guilty... I just left him in the muck of it all. I was too busy listening to everyone else. I ignored him because he was my son, and I thought he'd always be there. I assumed on some level that he knew how much I loved him, no matter how I acted. I loved him, would always love him. It turns out, of course, that children know you love them best when you actually have the courage to tell them...

"I watched him disintegrate, slowly... And do you know how I finally chose to deal with it? I put him on a list to be part of the next draft for Nepenthe-X, my own son, knowing the risks of what that entailed. I convinced myself it was the only chance he had of overcoming the depression. I think that's what it was. Maybe I just couldn't take watching his slow decay and wanted it done and over with, once and for all, no more suffering – just the Nepenthe... At least he'll never know the full extent of my betrayal...

"I came home last night and was greeted by my son's corpse dangling from a noose strung to a basement beam. The part that scares me most to think about is the careful premeditation of the act, the subtle preparations that he knew would be his last, like making a bowl of cereal or switching on the T.V. to check the weather. I think about the little green patio chair he grabbed from the shed. The rope he must have purchased at the hardware store with the few dollars left in his pocket.

The receipt saying 'Thank you for shopping at Hardware Plus, have a nice day'…

"HE must have paused to think about which wooden brace on the basement ceiling would be sturdy enough to carry his weight. Oh god, the test he must have done to see if it would work… I have this image in my head of my only son kicking and flailing his legs as he gasps for air and prays for me to come and rescue him. Realizing in a sudden panic how much he doesn't want to die and how stupid he was for going ahead with it."

WE were suspended in silence for a good while trying to soak in the professor's tears, trying to understand and forgive the man the way he needed us to, and not judge him as the fucked-up father that he was. "My son had a note tied to a keychain sticking out of his jeans pocket…"

SILENCE again, and then the professor's loud exclamation: "I won't let what happened to my son happen to the rest of you! I'm pushing on like Sisyphus now. I'll have my revenge. I'm ready to raise my fists in rage, even if nothing comes of it. But I'll need your help."

WE were all ready and willing.

"LET'S talk about practicalities. We'll need different groups completing different tasks. You three, come here." The rest of the room turned and stared at us as we made our way, embarrassed, to the front. "My son seemed to trust you, and you showed up here today without invitation, as if by chance… I'm afraid the onus of this task must fall on you." No pressure then… "This is a virus that will destroy the Nepenthe-X." He handed me a vial of plutonium-coloured snot then gave me a list of security codes and a non-napkin map of the building, with directions to the room in which the lotus was being held.

"THE rest of us will distract the guards and mislead as many other Department members as we can.

"WAIT until nightfall," the professor advised. "The guards change shifts at ten and the night patrollers are unenthusiastic about the severity of their charge in my experience."We nodded and tried to look serious and important, but unfortunately the professor chose that moment to take in our disguises for the first time, and the look on his face suggested he had finally realized just how low he had sunk by entrusting us with his confidence. Still he shook our hands before leaving the room, and at the last moment he handed me a folded-up piece of paper. My heart sunk. "I want someone else to see it," he pleaded. I pocketed Darius's note.

WE decided to head back to Cooter's place until we could enter the inner echelon of this maze-like laboratory at the professor's suggested hour, but first I ducked into a Coffee Time with the excuse of needing to take a shit. I locked myself into a stall that was only marginally more disgusting than the rest of that foul establishment and unfolded the emotional missile in my pocket with shaking hands. It read:

TO my dad: I've given this a lot of thought and decided that it has to be done... I remembered doing it and felt like anything other than how I saw it in my vision just wouldn't be right.

I tried to talk to you about my struggles, but you didn't want to think about a problem that didn't immediately respond to therapy or treatment. You couldn't bother yourself with the problem of living a human life. Can that one ever be fixed? You told me that I was worrying too much and that I should just forget about it and wait until a surer solution became available.

HOW is it that a father's profession can mean more to him than his only son's well-being?

THIS thing kept me up at night for weeks, because at the bottom of my heart I never wanted to do it. I wanted a life. A life with you.

I'VE tried to win your love and respect, even at the detriment of my own personal beliefs. Please know that I've done everything I could think of to win you over, Dad. Can you say the same about me?

I'M gonna give you one chance to make it up to me. I overheard you talking to that Department head about this new drug. I want it destroyed. If any part of you ever cared at all about me, you'll do this.

AT the end of it all, the only person I can really blame is myself. I know that now. I love you, Dad, I wish that was enough. For you and for me. I wish you the best of luck in dealing with your own dead end. I hope one day you'll realize there's no surefire treatment for dealing with death. I've finally come to terms with mine.

YOU'LL end up here one day…
– Darius Bakhshi

Twelve

"I Am that I Am..." – God

Skid marks in underwear
Biographers of vapid celebrities
Grins of suppressed bitterness

UNSETTLINGLY, Cooter, Remy and I had become the only ones capable of imposing self-awareness upon the world. We headed up the all-too-familiar fire escape and into the cesspit that had become like a second home to me. We were searching the cupboards for any miraculously unconsumed libations when we heard a shifty rustling from behind us. We turned and saw a gang of Department agents piling into the kitchen, clad in starched and stiffened uniforms which conveyed their uncompromising intentions.

WE were petrified. I tried to size up the brutes as they slithered past us. Then in waltzed none other than Ronald, our old Rectification leader, sporting a bruised jaw, still swollen and blue.

RONALD barged past us and announced, "You've missed your mandatory Rectification meetings and are therefore subject to detainment for evaluation. I have personally made it my mission to bring you back into the fold, Cooter, and the two of you will have to come along as well. Please remain calm, and hopefully we can avoid any unpleasant behaviour." Ronald said this last bit while rubbing his jaw.

COOTER and I looked at each other, trying desperately to gesture silent plans of escape. It wasn't going well and I was starting to feel panic take hold for the second time that day, when suddenly Remy screamed and jumped up on Cooter's kitchen table. "Yo, buds, it's me you want, ya fuckin' goofs! I'll do ya more damage than anyone! GAAAAAK!"

REMY proceeded to jump from tabletop to chair to kitchen counter, putting to shame any and every toddler who ever threw a tantrum. He was loving every moment of the anarchy. Ronald and the others didn't know who to pursue and stood frozen in thrown-off indecision.

REMY kept dancing. Then he darted for the window and screamed to me, "Throw me the snot juice!!!!"

I tossed the vial in the air and luckily Remy caught it. The stooges tried to grab him but the kid was too quick. Ronald screeched, "GET HIM! ONE OF YOU!"

IT was too late. Remy was out the back window and jumping over the neighbour's fence. The Department agents scrambled after him, and Cooter used the distraction to grab a plate and toss it at Ronald's head. Cooter and I ran down the front stairs and down the alley, and when we turned back we saw Ronald being accosted by the crackheads, I would have kissed each of their scabby, lice-infested heads if I could have. We ran as far and as fast as we could, ducking around the street corners of our glorious city until we felt sure that no one was behind us.

WE were safe. But Remy had the virus and now we had no idea where he was. I was proud of the kid's recent presence of mind but wished now that I'd kept the vial with me. It was hard to believe in Remy. We did whatever we could think of to reach him but to no avail. For all we knew, he could very well be in the hands of the Department, handing over our only chance to stop the machine. I comforted myself with the fact that they could have no way of knowing what was in that vial.

They'd figure on it being drugs, no doubt. Still, they'd probably confiscate it all the same…

EVERY time I tried to call him, the phone was answered by a Middle Eastern man named Gupta, and despite our valiant efforts to hurdle through the torrential tides of miscommunication, we made little progress. Gupta seemed kind at least.

WE resorted to roaming the alleyways as a dynamic duo. At one point we got to watch two wretched bums on a pair of motorized scooters thrashing at each other over a sautéed cigarette which ended up floating in a pond of street slime. The bums became increasingly violent and eventually began to use their vehicles as battering rams. Something about this majestic incident triggered an idea in Cooter's mind and he screamed excitedly, "I know where the kid's probably hangin'!"

COOTER tossed the hot-wheeling bums his pack of smokes as we left, a genuine act of true Christian charity.

AS we walked, I asked him, "Think he's still roaming free?"

"COUNT on it… one of the virtues of being a street rat is knowing how to squirm when things get hairy. He's dodged the authorities more than once, believe you me," Cooter jested, but I could tell he was worried.

THERE was this itchy sweat dripping off his brow, and he looked tense, perturbed and preoccupied by something beyond us both. I had to press, "You're looking jittery."

HE snapped, "Why the fuck you so interested all of a sudden? You got nothing but surrender written into ya, and all I ever hear ya talk about is how fucked we are or how there's no point… Sometimes I don't even think you're a Sanguinaire."

I yelled back, "And how the fuck do you decide who qualifies and who doesn't? Shit. Am I supposed to prove that I'm just as fucked up as you?"

COOTER'S reply sounded almost apologetic, and that terrified me. "I... just... never mind. Forget I said anything. I just meant that you're so closed off about there being any solution to this shit, but now suddenly you wanna tag along and help the professor try to botch the Nepenthe-X? A few weeks ago, you couldn't give half an ass skid of shit about any of this. It don't add up, pal. I need you to believe that we don't have to die the way it said we do... I need to know we're in this thing together, if you're even in it at all."

I tried to respond calmly, "Sure, I hold that things are a bit more fixed than you think, and you're right, I don't believe there's some kind of cosmic purpose behind the Event. But that shouldn't stop me from following this thing wherever it leads. I'm not that set on any one viewpoint. And what do I have to lose? No matter how I end up going, my life's been truly fucked by this thing. I'll always see my heart attack glinting back at me from my rearview mirror, so why not make a noise with you idiots? Cause a bit of damage if I can. I like the prof's Sisyphus angle. And I'm done explaining myself, so just you desist from questioning me."

COOTER looked cynical and asked, "What would ya do to stop this shit, then, if you're just tagging along to make a stink? How far would ya go?"

I answered, in all honesty, "As far as I have to, I'm in it now and I might as well go all the way. I'm in it for Darius, for his old man, hell, even for you, Cooter. We've all become friends, at least I think so... and you're the one who started it all. I've always kept people at a serious distance, but I gotta say, this past while it's been a relief havin' someone else to wallow with, to share a miserable laugh with, you know what I mean?"

COOTER nodded, but his face was grim.

I wanted to know why he was so insistent on scoping out my integrity. "Let me ask you, then, what's your stake in all this? You, the boastful Sanguinaire, working providence into every step of your drunken stagger. Lay it out for me once and for all. You think our visions were a warning or a test or what exactly?"

"FUCKING eh! Why else would we've had them? You gotta weigh the options. We know the Event happened, we know people had fucking visions, man, an' science can't explain it. Seems to me something else must have given 'em to us. Some powerful thing that we don't understand. So either it gave 'em to us 'cause it wanted to watch us suffer an' laugh at our misery, or else it could see we were fuckin' up these lives of ours and wanted to shake us out of it. Now if it's all just some fucked-up joke, then it's about the cruellest one I ever heard, but it doesn't do us any real harm to try an' stop the thing. And if we were given 'em as a chance to set ourselves straight, to join together an' focus on shit that matters, to prove that we can make our own choices and make 'em right, then we can't risk blowing it! Faith's gonna decide who wins this thing, man! People gotta be ready to lay down their lives. To make sacrifices. This is what it means to believe in something."

I looked down at the ground, feeling deeply embarrassed. It sounded like the sort of snake oil one would expect to be sold at a carnival. Cooter kept peddling his unwanted wares. "So you see, pal, I'm doing this for more than kicks. It means something to me. It's a chance to save way more than just our own lives; it's a chance to save all of fucking humanity."

I couldn't take any more and cut him off bluntly, "Alright! If there's any chance of me slipping out of my fate, I promise I'll pursue the possibility, and I sure don't feel like being drugged again… Our goals are in line, whatever our reasons may be. I'll give it all a go anyhow."

COOTER then asked me, "So you'd do anything to stop it, ANYTHING?"

"YEAH, I guess I would… I don't know what you're getting at."

HE looked at me with a smirk and said, "Who knows what kinda obstacles we'll run into, fella. But I guess I trust you. I'm starting to feel good about things again. Haha. Not you, though, eh? I can see it on your face. Not to worry, just follow me and you'll be alright..."

Thirteen

"I'M ON A HIGHWAY TO HELL!"

LOVE LETTERS FROM PEOPLE YOU DON'T LOVE ANYMORE
PROPERTY TAXES
THE GLOBAL ECONOMY

AFTER a half hour's walk or so, we arrived at Remy's potential hideout. The exterior of the building in question was filth-soaked, and you could see degeneracy engraved on its crumbling body. A broken sign that must once have flashed "Karaoke" in campy neon lights revealed that this was a bar and was the only evidence I could see that life had ever dwelled within these walls.

THE front window was doused in a hardened crust of scum that effectively prevented all light from peeping through its impenetrable gloom.

ON the barren front patio stood a pink plastic table with a gang of raspy-voiced forty- to fifty-year-old Yargers gathered around it. (Yarger is a term I've devised for a kind of Canadian hick. Its etymology derives from the *Yarrr-grrring* sound that is frequently uttered by this most prestigious caste of humanity). They were engaged in a discussion about hooch and the coming glory of their long-awaited welfare cheques, which a certain postman who was on the take would be delivering directly to this very establishment.

I stared in disgusted amazement at this group as they coughed, cackled and colluded their late afternoon away. They were clothed in the finest example of Yarger would-be swagger: a jean-on-jean getup from the early nineties topped with what must have been free giveaway beer caps and long, sweat-drenched hair protruding out from under the sides. My favourite of the three was a rotund sludge monster who had chosen to forego his hat in order to better display his long ponytail, which trailed beautifully down the back of his neck and around the sides of his cranium's bald centre. You could have made a casserole from the contents of his beard. All the combined crumbs and leftovers of his weekly feasts were nestled proudly in its folds. The sight of him helped to revive my spirits greatly.

I moved somewhat nervously to pass them, but then Cooter took on the role of Virgil and calmly led me through this first ring of Hades and past the broken-down entrance. It seemed like just the place Remy would be found: repulsive yet friendly. Several of the patron gargoyles gave me a welcoming salute as we descended slowly into their dung pit.

THERE we were, lurking in the bowels and digestive regions of Remy's hell, and there was Mr. Remy himself, standing happily at its centre. He was flailing around, tossing out cigarettes and slamming coasters, horking at every turn… He moved like one of those DDR dancers at the arcade, pushing, stomping, jumping and turning… All his movements were confined to one small orbit surrounding the pool table and its accompanying stools. He picked up a cue, a "shooting stick" as they called it, laughing and laughing and laughing…

I tried to soak in all of the atrocious atmosphere. I felt like a naturalist encountering a heathen tribe. Looking round, I saw a withered soul clinging to an oxygen tank, feeding quarters into a hijacked jukebox. Appropriately, the song he chose to put on repeat was none other than AC/DC's "Highway to Hell".

I then turned my attention to the rest of the patrons. There was beauty to be found in their every movement: the last cigarette shuffled through anxious fingers, the self-conscious tucking of a greasy strand of hair behind a partially torn-off ear. These were the reluctant and redundant gestures of lives unused and now unwanted.

OUR friend still hadn't spotted us and was slapping his knee and flicking matches, awaiting the next round of billiards so that he could defeat his ol' pal "Mickey", who I learned was the running victor in their little game of pool-roulette. Ultimately, one lucky champion would receive the honoured title of "Grand Pool Master" to laud over all the other half-living patrons. A momentous accomplishment exclusive to the Sunshine Tavern and available only to those sacred warriors inebriated enough to vie for the throne of ball and stick.

REMY turned and saw us at last, uttering a loud shriek as he did so. He approached us beside what they called a 'bar', which was in actuality a stripped piece of splitting wood superglued to a rattling ice box in which, Cooter informed me, they kept the booze… and other things. I imagined stashes of pickled eggs piled amongst various unnameable forgotten rot and paraphernalia.

OUR friend exclaimed, "Hey there, fellas! Shiver me shit fucks, Laertes, I never thought you'd make it out to a joint like this! Cooter, how'd ya get him here?"

"ONLY a mission from God could justify me bringin' him."

"YA, bud! Glad you made it outta yer place okay. Guess we should get goin' with the mission! We don't have much time…"

REMY'S Yarger friends were nagging him to get back to the game. He yakked at them to carry on the tournament without him. Cooter gave me a pointed look to make sure I understood how significant a gesture this was.

REMY reached into the only pocket of his drooping pants that didn't have a hole in it and scrounged around. His blackened hand emerged holding only crushed papers, a ripped, unused condom and some of the good ol' Nepenthe used for snorting. His face looked terrified and my heart was in my mouth, but then he reached into his shoe and pulled the vial out, beaming with pride, and tossed it to Cooter. He caught it and we both sighed with relief, then he frantically looked for a place to wipe his hand off, but soon realized that everything in the bar was sure to be even dirtier than Remy's shoe residue and gave it up.

I started questioning the kid, "So what happened to your phone? We tried calling you and this Bangladeshi guy picked up. It's been hell trying to track you down. I must say it was worth the trek, though. This place looks like it could host the cast of *Cheers* the way they look today..."

OFFENDED, Remy bucked, "YO, BUD! This here's my stomping ground... want me to knock your tooth out, bud? I had to ditch the fucking phone... Figured the Department can track that shit! Plus I'm tryin' to get away from the baby mama. She still won't stop calling... GAAAK!"

HE finished hacking up a lung then shouted towards the Asian woman standing behind the bar, "Judy! Fetch these scholars some drafts! Pickled eggs, boys?"

I couldn't contain my satisfaction. "I knew there'd be pickled eggs in there! Don't ask me how. But no, thank you, I think I'll pass this time..." I said, half-disappointed in myself for not being brave enough to taste that yoked mystery slime.

REMY returned, "More for me! Send 'em over this way, Jude! Hahaha, thanks!" Cooter joined in and munched away heartily, I suspect to make a point of identifying more with Remy than with me.

COOTER smiled as he suckled the last bit of egg and turned to Remy. "So you gonna tell us what happened or what? Did they tail you? Any close calls or grand escapes?"

REMY'S eyes flared and bulged, and he resembled a miniature youthful version of Rodney Dangerfield. "You bet, bud! You'll never believe this one. I ditched those fucks like in one o' them 1920s flicks yer always making me watch! The ones where the cops come runnin' after the robbers… always one step behind while I zipped ahead. It was a fucking hoot, bud! Those pricks don't know the streets like I do. Every dive's gotta special place fer' me just waiting… GAAAAK!!!!" Remy actually puked a bit with this heave of joy. "But that's not all I've bin up to…

"AFTER all my dashin' and dodgin', I get to thinking I deserve a pint for my efforts… But instead of hitting up this here paradise city where the grub is green and the girls ain't so pretty… heh… I went over to Lounge 457 across the way. There's always a good clam to shuck around those parts, harharhar. GAAAAAK!"

I repeated the name with curiosity, "Lounge 457?" A Yarger behind us seemed to overhear me and grunted with great disdain in our direction. Remy hushed me. "Don't say that so loud, bud... These guys don't like anyone goin' in there... It's like a code they got. You're not allowed to betray yer bar. They're very sensitive about these things.

"ANYWAYS," he whispered, "Lounge 457 is just across the street… they got real karaoke, not like the shit one here… and their meat isn't so recycled, if ya know what I mean…

Hahahaha, GAAAAK! I try not to go too much, though. Don't wanna offend my buddies, 'specially not ol' Mick." He pointed to a stumbling fiend who was wearing skintight Levi's jeans from the eighties and a leather vest with tassels hanging off the shoulders. "He's the cat I was just playin' pool with... A few months back, Mick and this other guy who works at Lounge 457 got into a real serious brawl. Not a pretty sight, bud. That pretty much drew the line about which side of the street you could hack a dart and drink a brew in."

IT didn't surprise me that these creatures had a rigid honour system in place. I wanted more details. "Who caused the fight, if you don't mind me asking?"

REMY lit a smoke right in front of the no smoking sign behind his head. Judy just sighed and lit one of her own, tapping the ash in an empty beer can. I laughed and looked back at my bard as he exhaled and began again, "Truth is, I'm not sure you'd understand, bud. The fuck from Lounge 457 called Mick a goof... and you *never* call one of these boys a goof, bud – talk about fightin' words! Anyways, Mickey smashed a beer bottle over the guy's head, GAAAAAAK!!!! Then Judy called the police. Mickey ducked the cops though, bud, hahahaha!"

I laughed. "Moronic heroism at its finest. I feel like I'm starting to understand these seedy characters that you call kin. But one thing confuses me: they act like Sanguinaires as far as the whole nothing to lose bit goes, but if I had to guess, I'd say they're all properly medicated. It's not the Event that's fucking with them, is it?"

REMY responded with great frustration, "Not everyone does everything just because they know how they're gonna die, bud. The Event isn't the only license to fuck yourself up. These guys aren't Sanguinaires, Laertes, they're doped up like the rest of 'em, but they've got just as much of a right to blow off life as you do. You make everything so complicated, bud, just chill sometimes…'

THAT was the first time I'd heard Remy use a completely serious tone, but he quickly returned to his normal self. "This isn't what I wanted to tell you, though. Listen how I spent the last couple of hours! Alright, so I'm wailing back a couple pints across the street, doin' some karaoke tunes on the ol' stage, when outta nowhere I see this tiny exotic Middle Eastern chick, drunk as a skunk, crying off in a corner. I walked over an' asked her what the matter was; I'm not such a bad guy, ya see? I couldn't make out what she said an' she just kept crying. I tried to buy her a drink but she wouldn't have any of it…

"SO I go over to the jukebox and put on the Village People's 'YMCA.' She smiled right at me, then boom! She starts making out with me. I'm like… whoa, bud, this is gettin' real hot real quick! It usually takes me putting the Prince on to get all the ladies after me!"

"I'M happy for you," I told him. "So did you lay with her?"

REMY happily boasted his proud reply, "Yep! Brought her right into an abandoned place next door. Oh boy, I slurped her oyster alright, two in the pink, one in the stink, bud, GAAAAAK! So afterwards this tiny girl just gets up to leave. I ask her if she wants to poke again sometime an' you won't believe the fucked-up answer she gives me! She goes, 'I got nine months to live, so if you wanna do it again, find me before then.' But she was smiling! And seemed tons lighter than when I first found her. Spooky shit, eh bud?"

NINE months, I mused… It couldn't be… "Did you catch her name by any chance?"

"SURE I did! A gentleman always knows the name of the prettiest girl he's ever porked. Her name's Fatima. Nice name, huh? She didn't look anything like the other floozies I dally with, 'bout as far as you can get from my beached-whale baby mama. You can't imagine how sweet it was."

I grimaced. "Shit, Remy. She went to our meetings."

COOTER nodded solemnly. "I hope it was worth it, pal." Remy looked confused for a moment, but he didn't care enough to ask, and we let it go…

Fourteen

The Arrest

Dirty handkerchiefs
Cheesy wedding vows
Emotional cheating

REMY took another swig, and the two of us followed suit after calculating that we still had about an hour and a half 'till we had to leave for the lab. But just as I was starting to feel comfortable in my scabby new surroundings, two husky Department agents came barging into our nest. They consorted with Judy and probably threatened to deprive her of her unlicensed tavern, because after a minute she pointed them in our direction. They looked like mall cops and carried with them a couple of batons and some handcuffs.

COOTER and I managed to duck into a booth before they spotted us, but they saw Remy and were on him like pit bulls, pulling him away. Judgment Day was here for the poor kid. Cooter and I just listened in horror – we couldn't risk getting caught with the vial – but Remy put up a brave fight.

"WHERE are you ponces takin' me and why? Huh, buds? So I missed a couple meetings, no big deal… No need to be so rough about it!"

ONE of the stout agents responded, "Stop resisting, Mr. Remington. Had you attended Rectification therapy, you would know that a new bill has been passed. Those who fail to attend Rectification are deemed untreatable by conventional means and are therefore subject to evaluation for a new form of treatment. Your continued refusal to attend your scheduled meetings constitutes consent to this evaluation. You must come with us."

REMY did not agree. "What the fuck are ya talking about? I didn't sign nothin'. Why don't you two just sit down and have a drink… It's on me. Eh, Judy… get these boys a round on me!"

THE vapid executioners dismissed Remy's attempt to placate them with three-dollar drafts and repeated, "Failure to attend your meetings now constitutes consent to evaluation for alternative treatment. Please come with us, sir. We want to make this easy for you; we know how confusing this must be, given your condition."

REMY wasn't having it. "This is bullshit, go fuck yourselves. I'm not going nowhere!"

"WE apologize, sir, but the Department has passed these regulations, and our actions are in accordance with a mandate we have received from the municipal police, who consider you to be a first-grade threat to the safety and well-being of others. Please do not make this difficult," concluded the agent.

THE second brute added, "As it stands, Toronto is on lockdown as we attempt to locate stowaway Sanguinaires. It would be in your best interest to cooperate with us. You may be able to mitigate your treatment if you are willing to provide information that leads to the location of other offenders."

WE had to get out of this situation… It was now or never. We began inching toward the door as they focussed in on Remy… Right as we got there, one of the agents barked for us to stop.

AS always, Remy came to our rescue. "Hey, Mickey," he shouted, "get Tracey and Saunders… these fucking mall cops wanna fight! Scout's honour! They're a couple o' fuckin' goofs with no authority! Get 'em, boys, they're tryna take me away!!!"

THREE Yargers from the patio heard Remy's call to arms and busted through the door just as 'Girls, Girls, Girls' began to blast from the jukebox. Mickey smashed a cue off the pool table, and with a sharp, jagged edge pointed right at the agents, he shouted, "Hey, ya fuckin' wannabe coppers! You causin' trouble for my bud Remy and his palz?! Well, this here'z gonna be a problem fer yer fuckin' skull!" He was brandishing the broken pool cue the way a wild caveman might wave his club.

REMY screamed, "Run, you fucks! Just go!!!"

IT was a bar brawl worthy of Patrick Swayze's Road House. It must be said for these Yargers, they have hearts of gold and nothing but hate for any kind of authority. Sadly we didn't have time to witness the outcome of this altercation. We were out and veering down Dawes Road as fast as our decrepit limbs would carry us, but looking back, we saw a huge crowd gathering around the tavern.

COOTER was running beside me and I heard him murmur, "Goodbye, Remy."

AND then there were two…

Fifteen

I am the Enlightened Cricket

Being unable to say no
Clogging someone else's toilet
Trading pot for sex

WE stopped running when we reached the creek and decided to waste time there until nine-thirty or so. There was plenty of foliage nearby which we imagined we could jump into, Scooby Doo-like, if we saw anyone coming.

WE sat slouched on a fallen tree that had served as a bench and bed for many a homeless wanderer, as evidenced by the residue of cigarette butts and empty beer bottles, and Cooter began writing something in a little journal he had pulled from his back pocket.

AS I rested there contemplatively, I noticed something strange in the little urban lagoon across from us. It was a loud, stinging buzz that wouldn't fucking stop. It rang with this loud, sharp, almost electronic sound, ripping through my ear. I couldn't gauge what it was at first but remembered having heard it thousands of times before. I figured it was maybe from a power line, but there were none around us. It was driving me mad.

AFTER several minutes of torture, I got up and followed the mystery noise to its source. What I found was a winged demon cricket thing. The fucker thundered out a colossal whine that reverberated all throughout the ravine. It was this little cricket asshole, responsible for all that deafening pain! That's what it was, a cicada! Not just in that instant but ringing ad nauseam throughout my entire woebegone life!

SOMETHING about this discovery made me feel almost normal. I was calm and at peace for the first time in a long time, just watching that stupid little thing as it hopped away. In a flash I understood the difference between the "afflicted" Sanguinaire degenerates I ran with and the rest of the world. There it was, the revelation I hadn't been looking for and felt sure I would never find. The thing I had driven myself insane trying not to realize…

THAT loud cricket stood in a celestial silhouette with an outline like Buddha must have had when he appeared to his Bodhisattvas. It just hit me – **mankind wasn't choosing to ignore the voice of its own mortality… mankind couldn't even hear that it was there. The annoying noise of life had blocked it out.** The daily distraction of living was, for them, so egregious that it prevented them from thinking or feeling about anything else. It wasn't their fault. How could they possibly appreciate the significance of the Event with the deafening clamour of life's chaotic bustle ringing incessantly in their ears? Life's bullshit rattle was just too overwhelming, and it didn't leave room for anything else.

I stood, thunderstruck, staring at Cooter as he wrote whatever he was writing, and let my revelation spin its course through my fractious and scattered brain. Wildly careening trains of thought went off in every miserable corner that it hit: maybe it wasn't a good idea to prevent Nepenthe-X from being produced. Maybe it was wrong to oppose this thing. If something so small could divert all my attention, all the concern I'd felt moments before about the Event, about being arrested, drugged, deprived of my identity, why not use a force that mirrored the insect's effect, only without such an annoying buzz?

I am the enlightened cicada.

MY cicada experience left me numb. I didn't dare share it with Cooter yet. I just returned to the rotting stump and sat beside him in silence, trying to think the thing through to its end. By and by I noticed Cooter sneaking suspicious glances at me like an addict protecting his stash. He was turning into an increasingly deranged animal, caged in his own inescapable mind. I felt chained to this inmate of a friend. But maybe my insect wisdom could set me free.

I debated trying to convince him not to go ahead with the plan, to reconsider the inescapability of things, to help him share in my newfound relief. I felt that it was my responsibility. I had to convince him to let get of it all. I had to show him that we could both be free if we embraced the distracting ignorance that the cicada, and maybe the Nepenthe-X, could offer us. Shit, was I Rectified? There was only one thing I knew for sure: I couldn't destroy the lotus.

I knew I had to tread carefully. Trying to seem as though nothing had changed, I turned to Cooter and asked, "What are you writing? You never put anything down. You should try breathing once in a while."

HE huffed back, "I'm almost finished. I'm just trying to get my head around this last little paradox."

I felt like he was being enigmatic for effect. I couldn't handle any more falseness. So out it came: "Listen, Cooter, I'm starting to rethink this thing. Look at us – we're hiding out in a fucking creek with a vial of god knows what, one friend dead, another fighting for his life, and an impossible mission with no promise of anything at the end of it. Let's say you're right, and we destroy the stuff, and people start fighting back and changing what they saw in their visions. What choice do they really end up with? They're going to die all the same, sooner or later. Humans have always known that, so what does it matter? Maybe the Event shouldn't elicit hopes of changing how we die; maybe it's a chance to accept and understand that we're going to go, a chance for a peaceful surrender."

COOTER looked like he'd just been punched in the stomach. He reeled for a moment and then said, "Say I pointed a gun at your head right now. Say I told you your vision was wrong 'cause I'm gonna shoot you right this second. Would you care? Would you just stay still an' smile like a dolt? No. Didn't think so. Now if that gun takes the shape of a heart attack, you think once you start nearing your end you won't feel the exact same as you would now if I threatened to shoot ya? You think you'll just whistle on a happy march to your own execution? You can't tell me that it's wrong to care, to feel something about how you're going to end up! You wanna deny people their right to feel and think that? You wanna deny me that???"

HE sobbed this last part. I listened calmly and replied, "Do I want to deny you false hope and a load of pointless pain? Ya, I think I do. There's no escaping this thing, Cooter. Look at Fatima. You heard her. She vows to stay celibate and ends up fucking Remy, of all people! But Remy said she was smiling after. Or Darius, for fuck's sake. He told me he'd never once thought about suicide before the Event, but once he'd seen it, he knew there was no escaping that noose. That knowledge did him in. But you should have seen the guy on his last day, man. That guy was calm. Cool as ice. He'd accepted it all and if he wasn't smiling, he certainly wasn't crying either. There was grace in his farewell. So if there's something behind this whole thing, then it's that. That chance to make peace with our end and not get so fucked up about it."

COOTER shuddered in angst at my newfound wisdom, "Are you taking that new medication or somethin'? Is your head getting all fucked up, muddled, unclear?"

HE couldn't shake me. "No, man, but maybe I'd like to be. Is it better to dread every moment of my life while I try to wrap my head around the inevitable? I just can't see that anymore."

COOTER put down his pad and pen, gazed straight into my soul and asked, "Are you seriously saying that oblivion is a viable alternative to life's struggles?"

"NO, Cooter, I just don't wanna struggle for no reason. Maybe if you could prove to me that someone, anyone, has ever managed to escape their vision. Maybe that'd make a difference. But I'm not even sure anymore. Maybe we're really fucked up and the Department's just trying to make our condition a little more bearable. Did you ever consider we might be mentally ill?" He was twitching and squirming in despair, but I kept going, "Hear me out. We're all unhealthy, alcoholic, unstable, suspicious, paranoid, miserable… and just plain hateful. Is that how a person should be? Think about Ezri. You had a real good thing there and you threw it away. And your job? I bet it's not the first one you've lost this year. Now let me double down and you see if I don't walk out a big winner. I bet you've always been this way. Am I right? Since even before the Event? You said you dreamed of becoming a plumber. Well, I call bullshit. You already were what you are now. Always jumping from job to job, woman to woman, no family and a mean case of self-loathing… Am I right?"

HE looked frightened now. "You and I are the same miserable kind, Cooter. We're cynical, selfish and hedonistic. Always have been, always will be. We're not the kind of people who could ever make a difference to anything. We're being kids about something as simple as death… It's time to grow up."

COOTER replied in a whisper, "So we just sit around, waiting for death to come a knockin'? We just welcome him in, scythe in hand? Oh hey, Death, can I get you anything? Beer, perhaps?"

I replied, "And what if it's not so bad waiting? What if there's a way to laugh while we sit out the ride?"

I could only just make out his reply. "Nepenthe-X? That's your answer?"

"MAYBE, maybe not. Anything's better than how it's been so far." I still had the cicada at the forefront of my mind.

COOTER made one last appeal. "What if I can prove to you that we can change our fate? What if I can *show you* that it's possible? That I can *change my vision*? Will you give me that chance, man? If I'm wrong, we do it your way. Just let me try?"

I nodded slowly. Cooter tutted and turned, annoyed. I knew he wouldn't accept anything but an audible and emphatic yes. That's just the way he was. So when he turned back again and looked at me expectantly, I gave him what he wanted. I had to. "Fuck it. Yes. But I warn you, once this shit's done, I might never want to see you again."

AND so we shook hands and started our ascent up the ravine's hillside. As we reached the top, we took a good look over the Danforth and saw smoke in the distance. The wailing of fire trucks and emergency vehicles could be heard not too far off, and as we got nearer to their symphonic alarms, we saw police swarming the streets. Something was very wrong…

Sixteen

D.P.W.-20

AGING
COLD WEATHER IN APRIL
BAD REMAKES OF CLASSIC MOVIES

WE were on the threshold of the pandemonium, unable to comprehend what we were seeing. In the past hour, the streets had become cannibalistic. Groups of protestors were rioting and setting things ablaze. We asked a gang of nearby kids what was happening. They looked at us incredulously. Then one of them pulled out a phone.

THE video he showed us was almost too much for me to handle. It was online. It had hundreds of thousands of views. And it was Remy…

THE kid's violent arrest had gone viral. We stared as our friend was beaten to a pulp on the four-inch screen in front of our eyes. We couldn't tell by the end if he was alive or not, but I doubted it. The comments were an ever-escalating set of horrified reactions. "The Department's gone too far!"

"WHAT if this was your little brother?" It was hard to believe that a moment we'd caught the first frames of in person had started the chaos on the streets before us. But so it was.

WE figured the flaming multitude of distractions pretty much guaranteed us safe passage to the lab, and we darted as quickly as possible in that direction.

THE rioters were becoming more and more volatile. We saw two police cruisers being pushed over, officers still inside, by a gang of scarved hoodlums. The Department agents ran everywhere, trying to supervise each encounter. Like the church of old, the Department aimed to guide the execution of justice but accomplished very little.

COPS started pouring out from around a nearby corner, and in an effort to avoid being nabbed, Cooter and I hurtled ourselves down into an open sewer-type thing. Remy's enchanting tale of incarceration, bull pit and all, echoed hauntingly in my ears, and for a moment all I cared about was avoiding arrest, even if that meant swimming through an ocean of shit. We waded a while then popped back up to the surface and decided to take the TTC to Queen's Park Station.

AS we huddled into the back seats of the train, a few Department agents raided the compartment. We sat hunched over, aiming for anonymity. Cooter started to whistle in a cartoonish attempt to seem innocent. I swatted him until he stopped. An announcement from the conductor rattled through the underfunded speakers, accompanied by an opera of crinkles and cut-outs which made it very difficult to understand the muffled voice trying to escape the void. "Attention all Toronto Transit Commission passengers, we are currently experiencing a delay at St. George Station due to an ongoing investigation. Do not be alarmed, there are D.P.W. agents and police officers placed at every station and throughout the trains. There is no cause for concern. Please remain calm. We apologize for any inconvenience. The TTC wants to ensure the safety of all its passengers. Thank you for your patience, and on behalf of the TTC, let me wish you all a wonderful day and a safe commute."

FOR the record, I hate the TTC. Many of the passengers were agitated, not because of the riots and protests but because they were late for whatever pressing after-dinner engagement was beckoning. They didn't seem to give half a shit about how or why the protests had started. All they cared about was that these riots were getting in the way of their banal routines, and with my newfound cicada enlightenment, I could kind of see where they were coming from…

WHEN you're entirely preoccupied with your own trivial triumphs and dissatisfactions, it can be hugely annoying if other people can't just shut the fuck up about things. After all, it's not like the important businessmen and women were forcing their affairs on the protesters, so why couldn't they just be decent and return the favour? At least I think that's how they'd see it. So I sympathized with their exhales of exasperation towards these overzealous groups, whose arguments they knew they'd already heard a thousand times before and so didn't need to listen to.

A second announcement came that the train was turning back at Bay Station, but luckily this wasn't far from our destination. We crept out of the filthy tunnels and ran until we found ourselves at Avenue and Bloor.

THE police were starting to assemble themselves in a tight phalanx formation, like ancient warriors readying themselves for the rape of a city. Droves of officers and Department agents barricaded Bloor, equipped with bulletproof shields and batons. It was nothing short of an improvised army called in from all across the Greater Toronto Area.

THIS pseudo-military front began marching towards campus, where most of the action was apparently taking place. The riots were well and truly underway.

WE couldn't much control the direction we were heading and had to weasel through whatever chinks we could find. Witnessing, as we went, the amalgamation of various different radicalized groups converging like fleets of ships readying themselves for battle in a cold and unforgiving sea, where no real mark or memory could be made because the other side didn't even care that it was happening.

THE rioters were wearing scarves and masks, which I gathered they'd acquired by pillaging Yonge Street. They were burning garbage cans and smashing windows with hammers, bricks and cinder blocks all the way down to Dundas. The streets left behind in this wake of violence were stained with smoke, glass and gutless hatred.

THE would-be army pushed back the violent gaggle. Cooter and I slipped through their ranks using the trusty alleyways, trying to keep ahead of the police, but this time we found ourselves right in the centre of the revolt.

IN the frontline of rioters was a kid with a face you just wanted to punch. Perhaps knowing this, he soon pulled a WWI gas mask over it. The little shit knew how to get a fight started and provoked the crowd to stand tall and hold their ground. He was carrying a hammer in one hand and a jagged, soot-covered brick in the other, screaming, "Come on, you fucking pussies! Let's fight!!!!"

I watched as the kid tossed the brick, which was soon followed by a barrage of catapulted fodder from his fellow companions, striking the front ranks of officials. The army backed off a bit and then returned with a volley of rubber bullets that demolished the first line of rioters and prodded the rest of them into a stampede that took Cooter and I by surprise.

MOUNTED officers adjacent with police cruisers began to cut off and close ranks around the group. Cooter and I saw them coming along Wellesley Street and hid in a small nursery playground as they passed us, as angels of death must bypass marked locations of innocence. Crouching down, we smelled the reek of burning tires and heard the sound of bones being shattered. We shared a look and made a dash for it, ducking bricks and rubber bullets. We saw small pockets of armoured officers accosting the protesters, stomping on their faces to ensure they had no teeth left – a necessary prerequisite of being arrested, to be sure.

BUT I hated the protesters almost as much. I hated this whole meaningless parade of discontent. These things always go the same way. They start out with a kernel of actual wrongdoing that quickly metamorphoses into some juggernaut of an issue, consuming and conflating all other offenses, real or imaginary, in its path. Be it an environmental problem, a health issue, a fucking dog leash permit bylaw, humans have this perverse need to drag out whatever cause they've picked up and beat it senseless, in mob-like fashion, with ever-growing support from every sulking whelp who ever fancied themselves offended, until finally their bitching amounts to an all-out riot.

AND when everything fouls up and the tear gas is flung into these self-declared downtrodden masses, the ones who started it all point fingers and vie for the exculpating status of victimhood…

BLOOD, screams and tears sprayed out from the blocked-off hordes of rioters behind us, but we'd made it through and were almost at the lab. We kept our heads down and ran.

Seventeen
Cleft's Way

Cathedrals with entry fees
Children who drown in their own swimming pools
Overcrowded homeless shelters

WE saw the professor from a distance, surrounded by a group of protesting students. He looked disgruntled and exhausted. He was glancing anxiously from side to side, holding out for our uncertain arrival.

"LAERTES! Thank God, you've made it! I don't know how much help we can be, but we couldn't have asked for a better distraction! Who would have thought it would end like this, eh? No time to lose! Off you go!" He said this just as Department agents began to close in.

THE professor stood his ground and tried to reason with the bloodhounds. Instead they kicked in his nose and then stomped out the rest of the features of his face, I actually saw blood get stuck in his eyebrows as we started to run. I was getting so tired of running...

IN an instant there were officers on our tail, and we knew we had to lose them before we could start to awkwardly navigate the lab with our map, so we led them away from the building and down a side street.

REMARKABLY, Cooter managed to coordinate his flailing body to seize hold of a cigarette which he actually got lit whilst running. He was coughing, smiling and smoking all at the same time, and we bolted as fast as our condemned corpses could take us.

THE goons behind us were gaining momentum, and I feared they'd either catch up to us or call enough attention to the chase that someone else would.

THEN, to our left, I saw a trash can with a banana peel slimily leaking out of its lid. Cooter's eyes glistened, and I feared what he was thinking. I knew his idiocy all too well and before I could stop him, he ran toward the garbage and grabbed the banana, with an idea of throwing it at the feet of the officers just behind him… I screamed, "You fucking idiot! No one really slips on banana peels!"

JUST as I said this, the moldy piece of decayed fruit gooped and oozed its way down Cooter's body, causing him to kick out in disgust and knock the entire can over, which miraculously worked to slow down our assailants. Then, as the officers began kicking through the trash, a group of campus police and smug liberal do-gooders joined forces and blocked our pursuers off in order to reprimand them for making a mess and, worst of all, for mixing the organics into the "coffee sleeve and lids pile" which was now cluttered together in a sordid mix, that of our salvation.

THIS whole incident gave us enough time to sneak into the lab unnoticed. The professor had highlighted the hallway that would lead us to the lotus, and after a bit of fumbling we found it. We used the professor's pass card and code to open the last door between us and our goal. Cooter was mirthful, and I had to give it to him, revolution or no, this whole adventure had been a ball!

Eighteen

Hiroo Onoda

Suicide

Seizures that the doctors say are unthreatening but ultimately kill you

Having your family member sleep with your loved one

I suppose surrendering isn't much of a loss if the war's been over for years and you were just the last to be told. I remembered reading about a Japanese soldier from WWII who dug himself in on an island in the Philippines and refused to surrender until the 1970s. His commanding officer had to come out of retirement in order to decommission him… After this the soldier became a successful public official…

I felt impossibly calm as we made our final approach toward the lotus. I hadn't known it could be like this. For a time there, I used to feel guilty whenever I took pleasure out of life. Guilt about being happy, guilt towards beauty, guilt just for smiling… But now I was serene. Instead of the racing mania of when it will happen, I felt the joy that came with recognizing that it hadn't happened yet…

WE walked to the back of the room. There it was. Blue, luminous and utterly defenseless.

"ALL this shit over that stupid fucking plant," said Cooter, staring unimpressed at the lotus in its incubator-type container.

"WHAT should it be over?" I asked him in return. "This much destruction probably can't be justified by anything. I'd say a flower seems as good a cause as any."

HE shrugged.

"WELL, Cooter, we're here. I'd say it's time to prove whatever you think you can prove."

HE snickered to himself. "Alright, fair enough. You want to know my vision, ya? Well, I'll give you a clue. I've seen that fire axe over there ten times a day ever since the Event."

I looked over in the direction he had gestured toward and sure enough, there was an emergency fire axe on the wall right beside me. My knees buckled.

"OH yes. Are ya gettin' it now? Here's another hint. I've watched that axe find its way through my head a thousand times over."

MY throat felt dry and I had to cough out the next word, "Me?"

HE nodded slowly, and his face had a truly maniacal look plastered across it. He was grinning from ear to ear. I felt sick.

"BUT..." I stammered, "but... why did you befriend me? If you thought I was your killer? Why the fuck would you do that?"

COOTER sighed, exasperated. "Christ, I thought you'd get it. I got to know you so that I might be able to convince ya not to kill me. See? I figured out fast that'd be the best way. I needed you here to prove it, though. You see now, right? You see how easy it is? We just eviscerate the plant and walk the fuck out of here. Boom. No more inescapability. Fuck, man, think about it! No part of me is supposed to carry on after this – that leaves my fate wide open to invent and create for myself!"

I marvelled at the complexity of this thing. How tempting it was now to believe that life had a higher purpose, that we could do something that mattered, that everything really was about *us*… I was swimming in sweat…

COOTER couldn't stand my silence, and I couldn't blame him. "What do ya say, pal? Let's lay waste to self-defeating medication. Fuck the oblivion, fuck the denial. Man, this thing's bigger than you or I. Let's do it for Darius, for Remy, for all of 'em."

I shuddered. I couldn't kill him. But I couldn't let him destroy the lotus either. Stupidly, I glanced at the axe that was right beside my head.

"I can see what you're thinking, you bastard!" Cooter howled, then, calmer, "Fuck it! Think away. I've done my part. You have to decide. I won't fight ya."

I yelled back, "I don't want to hurt you, you idiot, but I can't let you take away everyone else's chance at some peace! Let's just walk away and leave the plant alone. Everyone wins. You get free will. I get my medicine, and so do all the other wretched souls who don't know they need saving yet."

"WHAT happened to you, Laertes? You never gave a damn before, and now you're going to try and save them from having to live their lives, even if it means killing me?" Cooter pouted.

I replied, "I'm just so tired. I've made up my mind. I'm not gonna touch you, and you're not gonna touch that. C'mon, let's go."

COOTER stomped the floor with his feet. "I can't leave it here! Even if I escape my vision, who's gonna believe me if you won't back me up? They'll just keep druggin' everybody and none of it'll matter!"

HE reached in his pocket for the vial containing the virus and jolted towards the lotus.

"COOTER, don't!" I cried, panicked. I reached toward him and grabbed his wrist, but he pulled a rusty knife out of his pocket, no doubt in preparation for this inevitable moment, and sliced at my hand.

RAGE flooded through me like I'd never felt before. I turned and smashed the emergency glass. I grabbed the axe. He opened the top of the incubator, about to pour the virus in.

I yelled, "Don't do it, man. I'll have to hurt you!"

"I can't not."

I tried to hit him with the back of the axe but lost my grip on the handle, and the sharp metal split right through his head, dicing it open like a sacrificial offering. A single stream of blood flowed down his face. The virus spilled onto the lotus as the vial slipped from his fingers, and the flower immediately started to shrivel. The plant died in a matter of seconds as Cooter's body became limp, watering it with the trickling stream of blood from his head.

I saw the notebook sticking out of his pocket. I opened it. Scribbled in terrible writing, I read: "I have to stop this fucking jerk. It's almost too late… I gotta find a way…"

Epilogue

SITTING here now, I find myself reflecting calmly on what I used to hate most about everything... especially death... If you'd asked me then, I would have put it thusly...

IT'S not that you're shoved into a dirt hole while your friends and family wail in terror as they grasp that this silent lowering will be the last instant they will ever be in contact with you.

IT'S not the eternity of unapologetic absence that instantly ensues.

NOR is it the fungal infection of domestic disputes that pollute the final stage of your passing. Forget the forlorn faces that reek of hidden dismay as they scuttle languidly, complaining about the quality of the reception's hors d'oeuvres.

AND don't confuse them for those despondent sufferers whose scowls seem to suggest frustration at your fateful end – instead realize that they're only livid because someone they didn't know threw the first flower on your coffin but should have waited in line.

IT'S not the pathetic eulogies that seem to ejaculate every synonym for good without ever specifying an actual detail of who you were. It's not the priest's repetitious diatribe or catch phrase, "I know I never knew ----, but being here with you all makes me feel as though I truly did..."

IT'S not the compulsion everyone has to parade the greatest sorrow, so as to satiate this all-consuming hierarchy of dread, this standard baseline of devastation. Nor is it the opposite – the mute and dumbfounded who mirror the void that excretes itself from your descending casket.

IT'S not that the whole thing ironically reminds funeral attendants of the series *Six Feet Under*, unwilling as they are to accept that at this moment, death is actually happening sans the imitation.

IT'S not the godless or God-fearing.

IT'S not the children who couldn't give a shit because they're too young to notice that they even exist or, better yet, who play tag and snicker slithery filth into one another's ears about who's brave enough to kiss their cousin.

IT'S not the elderly who stand by in suspended silence, shocked at the daunting image of themselves staring back at them as they watch you take your turn and immerse yourself in the dirt.

IT'S not that you will never know how much you were loved or hated because you won't be present for the very moment that knowledge is both needed or appreciated. God forbid anyone assemble to acknowledge the virtue and fortitude of their loved ones while they continue to breathe...

IT'S not what leads you to your death, be it disease, suicide or accident, and it's not what you leave undone.

IT'S that you never *were* and you always knew it up until you weren't...